A scream tore from her throat when he came down on top of her

"Calm down. Damn it, it's me. Jake."

Leigh stopped struggling. A shudder moved through her when she realized who it was. At precisely the same time it struck her that every hard angle of his muscular body fit against hers with the utter perfection of a well-worn kid glove. Her body recognized his on some primal, instinctive level and responded. Breathing hard, trembling violently beneath him, she blinked the hair from her eyes, trying to make out his features in the semidarkness.

The sight of him hit her with the power of a hollow point bullet. Her heart dipped and then spun into a wild freefall. She stared at him, unable to move, a hundred emotions descending in a rush....

"Get off of me!" she cried.

OPERATION: MIDNIGHT ESCAPE

LINDA CASTILLO

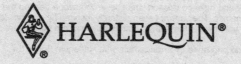

HARLEQUIN®

TORONTO • NEW YORK • LONDON
AMSTERDAM • PARIS • SYDNEY • HAMBURG
STOCKHOLM • ATHENS • TOKYO • MILAN • MADRID
PRAGUE • WARSAW • BUDAPEST • AUCKLAND

ISBN 0-373-88664-0

OPERATION: MIDNIGHT ESCAPE

Copyright © 2005 by Linda Castillo

This edition published by arrangement with Harlequin Books S.A.

® and TM are trademarks of the publisher. Trademarks indicated with ® are registered in the United States Patent and Trademark Office, the Canadian Trade Marks Office and in other countries.

www.eHarlequin.com

Printed in U.S.A.

ABOUT THE AUTHOR

Linda Castillo knew at a very young age that she wanted to be a writer—and penned her first novel at the age of thirteen. She is the winner of numerous writing awards, including the Holt Medallion, the Golden Heart, the Daphne du Maurier and received a nomination for the prestigious RITA® Award.

Linda loves writing edgy romantic suspense novels that push the envelope and take her readers on a roller-coaster ride of breathtaking romance and thrilling suspense. She resides in Texas with her husband, four lovable dogs and an Appaloosa named George. For a complete list of her books, check out her Web site at www.lindacastillo.com. Contact her at books@lindacastillo.com Or write her at P.O. Box 577, Bushland, Texas 79012.

Books by Linda Castillo

HARLEQUIN INTRIGUE
871—OPERATION: MIDNIGHT TANGO
890—OPERATION: MIDNIGHT ESCAPE

Don't miss any of our special offers. Write to us at the following address for information on our newest releases.

Harlequin Reader Service
U.S.: 3010 Walden Ave., P.O. Box 1325, Buffalo, NY 14269
Canadian: P.O. Box 609, Fort Erie, Ont. L2A 5X3

CAST OF CHARACTERS

Jake Vanderpol—Six years ago this MIDNIGHT operative sold his soul to bring down his nemesis— and it cost him the only woman he'd ever loved. Will he make the same mistake twice?

Leigh Michaels—She's running for her life from a killer who is obsessed with her. Can she trust Jake Vanderpol to keep her safe?

Ian Rasmussen—Escaped from prison, he doesn't care about running away. All he cares about is revenge against the woman who testified against him. The woman he'd once loved.

Sean Cutter—Burned out from twelve years of deep undercover work for the CIA, he is facing his first professional crisis as lead agent for the MIDNIGHT team. He must decide if Jake Vanderpol is a rogue agent or a godsend.

Mike Madrid—A master computer hacker with a shady past. He was the only agent who knew where Jake and Leigh had fled. Did he give up their location to Rasmussen?

Rick Monteith—Ex-cop turned rookie agent. He will do anything to prove himself. When the test comes, will he be ready?

Derrick LeValley—This deputy U.S. Marshal accepted a cool one million dollars and became a fugitive from the law to help Ian Rasmussen escape from a federal prison. Will he live long enough to spend the money?

Ronald Waite—The star reporter for a tabloid who agreed to help the MIDNIGHT agency with a sting. Will he reveal his anonymous source under torture?

Prologue

Facing the bitter November wind, convicted international arms dealer Ian Rasmussen gazed at the bleak Missouri countryside. He breathed in deeply, savoring the sweet tang of freedom after six brutal years without it.

The semi's diesel engine idled on the other side of the rest area, rumbling like thunder. According to the driver's logbook the truck's shipment of Italian furniture would be delivered to a furniture warehouse in Denver that very night. What the logbook didn't reveal was that a hidden room had been built in the front section of the rig's trailer—a ten-by-four-foot room complete with heat, a fully stocked wet bar, television set, satellite phone and a leather recliner.

Even on the run from every law-enforcement organization in the Midwest, Ian Rasmussen liked to travel in style.

Shivering with cold, the driver stood outside his door, smoking a cigarette. The passenger door swung open and Derrick LeValley, former deputy marshal, stepped out into the gray light of dusk. For a cool million dollars, Rasmussen had bought him off. The price had been steep, but worth every penny.

"I'm sorry, Mr. Rasmussen, but we have to go. The feds are expanding their search as we speak. It's best if we keep moving until the situation cools down."

Rasmussen turned to LeValley, who, just five hours ago, had walked into the Terre Haute Federal Prison with fake transport papers and had exited with him. LeValley had then taken him to this big rig and they'd been driving west ever since.

"I want to see the list," Rasmussen said.

LeValley reached into the pocket of his coat and withdrew the computer printout. "You don't know what it took to get my hands on this information. It cost a man his life. You owe me another fifty thousand."

"You'll get your money," Rasmussen snapped, then turned his attention to the list. "How many names?"

"Two hundred plus."

"Excellent." Holding on to the printout that listed the new identities and addresses of over two hundred witnesses from the Witness Security Program database, Rasmussen felt a heady rush of power. There were a lot of people who would pay top dollar for this information. But he was only interested in one name. He flipped to the second page, his eyes scanning, seeking...

Leigh Michaels.

Her name was highlighted in yellow. Beneath it, her address had been underlined in blue ink—345 West Fourth Street, Apt. 310, Denver, Colorado.

Kelsey James was now Leigh Michaels.

She could change her name, but she couldn't hide...

He ran his thumb over the name, and the old emotions began to churn inside him. Love that had putrefied into something darker than hatred. She had been a nobody when he'd met her. A waitress earning next to nothing. He'd taken her in. Given her everything a woman could ever want. He'd trusted her, loved her. He'd offered her his heart; she'd taken his soul. She'd thanked him with treachery, betrayed him in every way a woman could betray a man.

Now, if it was the last thing he ever did, he was going to make her pay.

For a dangerous moment he considered calling her. He wanted to hear her beautiful voice tremble with fear. He wanted her to know he was coming for her. She deserved to suffer, the way he'd suffered for six torturous years.

"Mr. Rasmussen, we have to go." Derrick LeValley went to the cargo door and opened it.

Rasmussen folded the list and walked to the rig. "You have someone watching her?"

"Since yesterday. She's on the move, but they've got her covered."

"I want to be in Denver by dark."

"We're right on schedule."

Rasmussen climbed into the trailer and headed toward the hidden room. There was much to do, but he couldn't do any of it until he dealt with Kelsey. She came first, above all else. Only then could he think about the rest of his life.

He entered the hidden compartment. Sweat slicked his back when LeValley closed the door behind him. The old claustrophobia descended. But even sweating and shaking, he was aware of the list in his pocket, of her name taunting him with the promise of sweet revenge.

By nightfall he would have her in his sights. He would come down on her so fast she wouldn't even know what hit her. Then he would take his time with her. He would make her pay for what she'd done. He closed his eyes, an image of her coming back to him with painful clarity. She'd been so innocent. So incredibly lovely....

Kelsey...

She'd cost him more than any man should ever have to pay. Six years of violence and humiliation. But sending him to prison wasn't the worst of what she'd done. His lovely Kelsey had not only betrayed his trust, but his heart. She'd given her body to another man. A federal agent. The very man who'd destroyed his life. No woman did that to Ian Rasmussen and lived to tell about it.

Not even the most beautiful woman in the world.

Chapter One

Jake Vanderpol didn't like surprises, especially nasty ones that came via his secure phone line in the middle of the night courtesy of the MIDNIGHT Agency.

"We've got a Code Red. All available agents report to duty ASAP. All unavailable agents are on standby. I repeat, Code Red…"

That was only the first in a series of bad news events. At 5:00 a.m. he was on the road and heading toward the MIDNIGHT Agency headquarters located in a small, nondescript building just west of Washington, D.C. A news junkie, he'd heard about the escape of Ian Rasmussen on the radio and just about ran his Hummer off the road.

By the time he swung the vehicle into the underground parking lot and jammed it into a reserved spot, he was on edge. He couldn't stop thinking about the young woman who, six years ago, had helped him nail the international arms dealer. It was the one and only time Jake had ever gotten personally involved with a witness. The one and only time he'd ever crossed that line. A line that in the end had nearly cost him his job.

Even after all this time, he still saw her face when he closed his eyes. He still smelled her perfume mingling with the sweet scent of her skin. He still dreamed of her—hot, sweaty dreams that left him hard and aching and full of regret. Worse, he still wanted her with a ferocity that shook him to his core.

He'd chalked up more mistakes in the one week he'd known her than in his entire career. She made him crazy, and he'd nearly thrown it all away. But in the end, when it had come time for her to walk away and start her new life, she hadn't looked back....

Shoving thoughts of the past away with the resolve of a man who did it far too often, Jake shut down the engine and hit the ground running. The MIDNIGHT Agency headquarters was lit up like a football stadium. At the front entrance two armed security officers nodded curtly when he flashed his badge. Rather than wait for the elevator, Jake ducked into the stairwell and took the steps two at a time to the third floor.

The instant he entered the hall he could hear voices coming from the "war" room. It was a large conference room that was transformed into a command center whenever there was a crisis. Jake figured the escape of a violent international arms dealer qualified as a crisis and then some.

He entered the room without knocking. All eyes swept to Jake. Four MIDNIGHT operatives sat around an oval conference table covered with paper. Two laptops were connected to a printer that was spitting out more paper.

Fellow operative Mike Madrid looked as if he'd been dragged from his bed, flogged and hastily dressed. A computer software hacker by trade, he was working on a laptop with one hand, gripping a cup of coffee with the other.

The two other agents in the room, Zack Devlin and Rick Monteith, didn't meet his gaze, and Jake realized there was a reason he'd been the last team member called. That reason ticked him off.

"Looks like I missed the party," Jake said to no one in particular.

The room went silent and tense, as if someone had tossed in a grenade and the agents could do nothing but wait for the explosion. Jake wasn't sure if the impending confrontation would qualify as an explosion, but it was definitely going to be loud.

They shifted uncomfortably in their chairs, averting their eyes. Coffee was sipped, fingers drummed, pencils tapped.

The agency chief, Sean Cutter, sat at the head of the table, his blue eyes cold when they fastened on Jake. "This briefing is over," he said.

Jake ignored his fellow operatives as they filed from the room. "Rasmussen is out and you didn't bother calling me, damn it."

"I've assigned other agents. They're capable and—"

"This is my case."

Cutter's eyes flashed. "This is whomever's case I see fit to assign it to."

"I built it from the ground up—"

"You slept with your witness!" Cutter snapped. "You screwed it up and I have no intention of letting you do it again."

"You know I'm the best man for the job," Jake ground out.

"I know you're too personally involved to be effective."

Jake's heart was pounding. He wanted to believe it was anger ricocheting through his body. But he could feel the fear pumping through him with every frenzied beat of his heart. He didn't want to ask about Kelsey. He didn't want to think about her or feel anything for her. But he did, and those emotions were tearing him up. He had to know if she was okay. Every agent who'd been in that room knew Rasmussen was going to go after her. He couldn't bring himself to think about what would happen if he found her.

"Is she all right?" he asked.

"As far as we know."

"What the hell do you mean as far as you know?"

The other man's jaw flexed and Jake got a sick feeling in the pit of his stomach. "This is bigger than just Kelsey James," Cutter said.

"What are you talking about?"

"Someone hacked into the Witness Security Program database."

Disbelief and a deeper, darker fear reared inside him. "No way."

"This hacker has names and addresses. Every agent I've got is scrambling. Every witness who's ever gone into the Witness Security Program is in danger. We're trying to prioritize, but how the hell do you prioritize when you have more witnesses than agents?"

Jake felt as if he'd been punched. "Rasmussen?"

"I don't know, but the timing of it points to him. He certainly has the resources."

He stared at his superior, his mind reeling as the repercussions of what he was being told hit home. "Where's Kelsey James?"

Cutter looked away.

"For God's sake, you don't know, do you?"

"I had an agent check her apartment as soon as we heard. CNN just broke the news. She must have heard about Rasmussen and left before we could make contact."

Jake swore. That sounded like Kelsey. Headstrong. Stubborn. Willing to take on the world all by herself if she had to. But she had to be running scared, and with good reason. If Rasmussen got his hands on her...

The thought made Jake break into a cold sweat. His protective instincts kicked in with a vengeance. "At this point it's probably safe to assume he has her name and address."

"This is not your case, Jake. I need you here. There are administrative—"

"Screw administrative!" Another curse burned through the air. "I'm not going to let him get her, Sean."

"I've got another agent en route."

"Come on! You've got two hundred federal witnesses to protect and twenty agents! Do the math!"

"We're working with the U.S. Marshals Service to contain all the witnesses."

Jake cursed.

"I need you here, Jake. But I need your head screwed on straight. If you can't keep it together you need to walk away."

"I'm not going to let him kill that young woman," Jake ground out.

"She knew what she was getting into six years ago."

"She knew. But so did we, didn't we, Sean?"

"Don't go there, Jake. You did your job, and so did I."

"Yeah. Maybe a little too well." Jake scrubbed a hand over his face, a harsh sound breaking from his throat. "Where is she?"

Cutter stared at him, his face as hard as a piece of granite. "Don't make the wrong decision, Vanderpol. I covered for you last time this woman got under your skin. I won't do it again."

"Is that the way this is going to go down?" Jake asked.

"That's the only way this can go down."

Never taking his eyes from the other man's, Jake removed his MIDNIGHT identification from his wallet and laid it on the conference table. Reaching beneath his jacket, he withdrew his government-issue service revolver and laid it next to the badge.

"Now you don't have to cover for me," he said, and then walked out the door.

A SLATE-GRAY PREDAWN SKY spat sleet as Leigh Michaels lugged her suitcase into the second-floor motel room and locked the door behind her. Fear had been her constant companion since fleeing her apartment in Denver.

She'd always known this terrible moment would come. Rasmussen was too powerful a man, his resources too far-reaching for any prison to contain him permanently.

Shaking, Leigh pulled the sleek H&K semiautomatic pistol from her waistband and set it on the night table, within easy reach. She didn't bother unpacking, because there was always the chance she would be leaving quickly. She didn't want to have to leave behind what few clothes and toiletries she owned.

She walked to the television and turned it to a cable news channel, hoping to hear that Rasmussen had been captured. The anchor immediately dashed her hopes. "An unidentified source has informed us that the database of the Witness Security Program was hacked into over the weekend. Over two hundred names of high-level federal witnesses have been stolen…."

Leigh felt each word like a vicious punch. For an instant she couldn't catch her breath, couldn't think. She could feel the terror building inside her.

Ian Rasmussen had to be behind the theft of the database records. Even if the television wasn't reporting the connection.

"Oh, God." Standing abruptly, she put her hand to her stomach and choked back a sound of pure terror.

Ian Rasmussen knew her new identity. He knew her name. Her address.

For an instant she considered calling her old contact at the U.S. Marshals Service office in Boulder. Then she remembered what had happened the last time she'd put her trust in a government agency and nixed the idea.

The image of Jake Vanderpol flashed in her mind. She saw dark, intelligent eyes. Military-short hair. A lean face and chiseled mouth. A body as hard and breathtaking as the Rocky Mountains themselves.

She'd trusted him with her life. She'd given him her heart. Her body. A piece of her soul. He'd taken all of those things with a ravenousness that had left her half-crazy with the need for more. She'd fallen hard for the brooding agent. But the intimacies they'd shared hadn't been enough to keep him from using her as a means to an end.

Shoving the memory back into its deep, dark hole, Leigh sat down hard on the bed and put her face in her hands. "Calm down," she whispered into the silence of the room.

There was no way Rasmussen could have tracked her here. She'd been too cautious, watching out for cars traveling too close. She would have remembered seeing the same vehicle twice. No one had followed her.

Still, she knew it was best if she didn't stay too long. She needed to keep moving. Once she'd put enough distance between her and Denver, she would stop in a new city, create a new identity, start a new life. It was her only hope of staying alive.

All she had to do was stay one step ahead of Rasmussen.

Glancing at the alarm clock on the night table next to the bed, she sighed. It was almost 7:00 a.m. She'd been driving most of the night. She needed a shower. Food. A few hours of sleep. Then she would hit the road again. If all went as planned, by tomorrow she would be in Kansas City. A place where she had no ties. No one had any reason to look for her there. All she had to do was stay alert and be cautious.

Feeling the hard tug of exhaustion, Leigh lay back on the bed, not bothering to take off her clothes or boots. The H&K was within easy reach, and she had a knife in her boot as backup in case she was caught unaware. But she didn't think anything would happen. No one knew she was here.

But as sleep overtook her, it occurred to her that she'd underestimated Ian Rasmussen once before, and it had cost her more than she ever could have imagined.

LEIGH JOLTED AWAKE. Lying on her side, she remained perfectly still, listening, her heart pounding. The room around her was cold and silent and dimly lit. The clock on the night table told her she'd been asleep just over an hour. What the hell had wakened her?

In the past six years Leigh had learned to trust her instincts. Right now those instincts were telling her something was wrong. She could feel gooseflesh racing along her arms.

The doorknob squeaked. She sat up, her heart hammering like a piston in her chest.

A second later the door flew open and banged against the wall. A man looking to be as large as a mountain in the semidarkness of the room rushed in. She scrambled across the bed, her hand groping for the H&K on the night table. A dozen scenarios rushed through her mind as her hand closed around the grip. No time to think. Aim and fire, just like at the shooting range where she'd practiced so many hours in preparation of this terrible moment.

She brought up the gun, swung the weapon around. An instant later, a strong hand clamped around her wrist. "Drop it," came a growled command.

But Leigh knew if she let go of the gun she was as good as dead. She screamed when he squeezed her wrist. "No!"

A gunshot exploded. Plaster rained down from the ceiling. She fought for control of the weapon with all her might, but even with all the self-defense classes she'd taken in the past six years she wasn't prepared for the strength and speed of her attacker.

A final, painful squeeze to her wrist and the gun clattered to the floor. The last of her hope fled as she heard the intruder kick it away.

He's going to kill me, she thought.

Knowing she had to act quickly if she wanted to live, Leigh used her free hand to reach for the knife in her boot. She'd barely gotten her fingers around the rubber grip when he locked both her wrists in his hands and shoved her back onto the bed. She tried to knee him, but he twisted aside just in time then came down on top of her.

She lashed out with her feet. But he was heavy and strong and overpowered her with ease.

"Calm down, Kelsey. Damn it, it's me. Jake."

Everything inside her froze at the sound of the all-too-familiar voice. Leigh stopped struggling, her body suddenly recognizing his on some primal, instinctive level. Every hard angle of his muscular body fit against hers with the perfection of a well-worn glove.

Breathing hard, she stared at him, unable to move, a confusion of emotions descending in a rush.

He glared down at her with dark eyes. His thin nose looked as if it had been broken and never properly set. His chiseled mouth was pulled into a grimace. But she knew from experience that his mouth could be gentle, too. That it could kiss a woman senseless if she wasn't careful....

"Get off me!" she cried.

His nostrils flared with every labored breath. He was staring at her as if she were a ghost and he couldn't quite believe he was seeing her. "Just be still," he said. "Don't fight me. You know I won't hurt you."

But Leigh knew that was the one thing Jake Vanderpol did exceptionally well. Something she would not let him do again. "You have no right to be here. To break into my room—"

"I'm here to save your life," he cut in. "If you're as smart as I think you are, you'll let me do it."

Chapter Two

Jake knew better than to think of how good she felt beneath him. She was a witness desperately needing protection. At least, until Rasmussen was captured or the U.S. Marshals Service could take over. But when it came to Kelsey James, the logic and the good sense he'd always prided himself on never so much as entered the picture: not six years ago when he'd crossed too many lines to count; not now because he had a pretty good idea that he was going to be crossing even more.

Staring into her vivid blue eyes with her body warm and soft against his, he prayed he could keep a handle on things this time.

Not bloody likely.

Feeling his body harden the way it did every time he so much as thought of her, he shifted, then pushed away, rose and offered his hand. Ignoring him, she scrambled across the bed and jumped to her feet.

"How did you find me?" she asked.

"I make a living finding people," he said. "Give me a break."

Her gaze flicked toward the door, and he realized for the first time how badly he must have frightened her. But he hadn't had a choice. He'd known that if he'd taken the time to knock, she would have gone straight out the window.

"Do you have any idea how close you came to getting shot?" she asked.

"The day you can get the drop on me is the day I deserve a bullet." He crossed to the door, looked both ways, then closed it and locked it. "Why didn't you call your coordinator at the U.S. Marshals Office? Let them relocate you, protect you until that son of a bitch is caught?"

"In case you missed the news, it was a deputy marshal who helped him escape. Someone inside the U.S. Marshals Office gave it up, Jake. How can you expect me to trust them with my life?"

Wishing he could dispute that, he strode to

the window, parted the curtains and surveyed the parking lot.

"What are you doing here?" she asked.

He turned to her. "I'm going to take you to a safe house."

"I don't want to go to a safe house. I sure as hell don't want to go with you."

"You don't stand a chance of surviving on your own. It's only a matter of time before Rasmussen finds you. We both know what will happen when he does."

A tremor went through her. "He won't find me."

"Don't bet your life on it. If he can hack into the Witness Security Program database, finding you will be a walk in the park."

"I know how to disappear. A new name. A new city. I can do it and I don't need your help."

Pulling the Glock from the shoulder holster beneath his coat, he checked the clip, then shoved it back into its leather sheath. "You were in the database. He's got your new name. Your latest address. As far as we know he could have had you under surveillance for quite some time."

"I know how to take care of myself."

"Not when it comes to Rasmussen."

She walkēd around the bed and got in his face. "I don't want you here. I don't need you. I don't need your help. I can sure as hell do without your brand of protection."

The words stung, but Jake didn't let himself react. He figured he'd had that one coming after what happened six years ago. He'd never forgiven himself for not getting to her in time to keep her from going back into the lion's den...

He may not have seen her for six years, but he'd kept track. She might think she was prepared, with her brown belt in karate and handgun training, but there was no way she was equipped to handle this on her own. She might talk tough; she might even look tough. But he saw the fear in her eyes. He doubted she had a clue what six years in a cage could do to a man like Rasmussen.

"I just want to help you," he said. "Let me take you to the safe house."

She stuck out her chin. "Or maybe you think I'm your ticket to Rasmussen. Maybe you want a repeat performance of how things went down the last time. You got that promotion after you nabbed him, didn't you? Isn't that what this is all about? Your ego? Your job? Get your man at any cost, including your own soul? Or in that case, it was my soul, wasn't it?"

Jake just stared at her. He wondered if she really believed what she was saying. If she really hated him that much after everything they'd been through. If she remembered as keenly as he did that not everything that happened between them six years ago had been bad.

"All I want is to keep you safe," he said. "I figure I owe you that much."

"Forgive me for not believing you, but that's the same thing you told me last time. Right before you used me."

That she could believe that about him made him feel like a son of a bitch. Six years ago his decision to use her as bait and set a trap for Rasmussen had occurred *before* he'd spent a week in that safe house with her. Before he'd touched her. Before he'd kissed her. Before he'd slept with her. Long before his heart had gotten involved....

In the end she had been the one to carry out the plan—without his blessing. To this day he didn't know what she'd had to do to get the goods on Rasmussen. That burning question had been tormenting him for six years.

Jake scrubbed a hand over his jaw. "You went behind my back—"

"Sending me to Rasmussen was your idea," she said.

That much was true. "I tried to abort the sting."

Her smile was cool. "You were too late, though, weren't you?"

"You were angry when you found out about the plan," he said. "You get reckless when you're angry."

"We both got reckless, wouldn't you say?"

He didn't know what she'd had to do to get Rasmussen to fess up on tape. He didn't know if she'd had to compromise herself… or worse. The only thing that was crystal clear about any of this was that she blamed him.

Jake bore that blame like a lead weight.

"Damn it, Kelsey—"

"Don't call me that. Kelsey James no longer exists. My name is Leigh." She glanced over at her suitcase. "I have to go."

Jake clamped his jaws together and struggled for patience. "Let me take you to the safe house." He stepped toward her. "I mean it. I don't want to see you hurt."

"I'll take my chances with Rasmussen. At least with him I know where I stand. He might be brutal, but he's a straight shooter."

The words slashed like a knife. Leigh Michaels was no longer the twenty-one-year-old farm girl she'd been six years ago. She'd blossomed into a stunning beauty with the street smarts of an undercover cop. The hard knocks she'd taken showed in her shadowed eyes. In the mouth that no longer smiled so readily. But she was still so beautiful it hurt just to look at her, and Jake felt the pain of it all the way to his bones.

Rounding the bed, she picked up the H&K he'd taken away from her earlier. With the ease of a woman who knew how to handle a firearm, Leigh checked the clip, then sheathed the weapon in her waistband. She walked over to her single suitcase, picked it up and started toward the door.

Before opening it, she turned and looked at him. Her eyes slid down his body. She hadn't meant the slow perusal in a sexual way, but he felt her gaze like the soft caress of fingertips over sensitive skin and his body jumped in response.

"Don't try to come after me, Jake. I know what I'm doing."

"You're making a mistake."

"It's not the first one, is it?"

"Could be your last." He watched her, wondering if any shred of what she'd felt for him six years ago was left inside her. "Don't do this, Leigh. You're going to get hurt."

"I've already been hurt." She smiled, and for a moment looked very much like the lovely young woman he'd fallen for six years ago. "See you around, Jake."

She slipped through the door.

For several eternal seconds Jake stood next to the bed, his heart heavy with dread. There was no way he could let her walk away. No matter how careful she was, Rasmussen would find her, and Jake knew what would happen when he did. The thought sickened him.

Leigh might not want to be protected, but there was no way he could stand by and let her do this. Even if he had to use physical force. It was a route he hadn't wanted to take, but the alternative was infinitely worse.

"Go get her, you damn fool," he muttered, and started for the door.

CLUTCHING HER SUITCASE, Leigh started down the hall at a fast clip. Her heart was still wildly pounding from the shock of seeing Jake again. She couldn't believe he'd found her. Couldn't believe the old feelings were still there, when she'd spent so many years trying to exorcise them from her system.

The doors on either side of her blurred as she broke into a run. She wasn't sure why she was running. Away from Jake and all the memories and feelings she'd struggled for so long to leave behind. But she knew that no matter how fast she ran she would never be able to outrun them.

She was midway to the stairs when a

man rushed out of the alcove where the ice machine was. Leigh darted left, but he plowed into her with the force of a Mack truck. The impact sent her reeling. Her suitcase flew from her grip. Then his strong arms locked around her and spun her around.

She caught a glimpse of long hair pulled into a ponytail. Eyes full of violence. She reached for the H&K in her waistband but wasn't fast enough. His hand shot out like a snake. Viselike fingers closed around her wrist and Leigh dropped the pistol.

"Try something stupid again and I'll kill you."

Leigh tried to twist away, but he slammed her against the wall. Pain radiated up her spine. Her scream was cut short when he slapped his hand over her mouth.

"Don't make a sound or I'll put a hole in you so big it'll take the cops a week to find all the pieces." He backed up the threat by jamming a pistol against her ribs. "You got that, pretty lady?"

Leigh jerked her head once. She just knew he had to be one of Rasmussen's thugs.

Setting his forearm against her throat, the man glanced both ways. "You alone?"

She nodded, wondering where Jake was. "What do you want?"

"There's a hefty pricetag on that pretty head of yours. Nothing personal, but I'm going to cash in."

She cringed as he ran his hands swiftly and impersonally over her body. She prayed he wouldn't find the knife in her boot.

Relief surged through her when he stepped back without patting down her calves. "We're going to take the elevator down. Nice and easy and quiet. You got it?"

He stepped into the dim light of a wall sconce, and she got her first good look at him. He was the size of a woolly mammoth with eyes so pale they looked white. His face was pocked and angular. He wore an expensive trench coat. And he held a deadly looking semiautomatic pistol aimed at her heart.

"Where are you taking me?"

"You'll find out soon enough." He jabbed her ribs with the gun. "Start walking."

Leigh glanced down the hall, but the door

to her room remained shut. Jake was nowhere in sight. It suddenly occurred to her he might not have heard the commotion. That he could have been on the phone with his superiors. Or maybe he was going to let this man take her and lead him to Rasmussen....

She knew it was stupid considering this man could kill her at any moment, but the thought hurt the same way it had hurt her six years ago. Damn Jake to hell. She didn't need him or his protection. She still had the knife, after all. All she had to do was wait....

The man motioned toward the elevator at the other end of the hall. "He wants you healthy, so don't try anything stupid."

Leigh's legs were shaking so violently she could barely put one foot in front of the other. Dizzy with fear, she started toward the elevator.

Rot in hell, Vanderpol, she thought as she passed by the door to her room.

But as much as she didn't want to admit it, she'd been secretly hoping Jake would burst from the room and save her. That hope dwindled as they neared the elevator. Leigh could take care of herself, but she was smart enough to know when she was out of her depth. The men who worked for Ian Rasmussen were in an entirely different league altogether. One that was vicious and deadly.

She was ten feet from the elevator when the sound of steel against steel stopped her. *Jake,* she thought, and spun. Her legs went weak when she saw him standing just twenty feet away, his weapon trained on the thug.

Snarling a profanity, the thug jerked her close and jammed the muzzle against her temple. "Make a move and I'll splatter her brains all over you."

"Drop the weapon and let her go," Jake said with icy calm.

The thug backed toward the elevator, dragging Leigh with him. "I don't think you're in any position to make demands."

Jake stepped toward him. "You hurt your precious cargo and Rasmussen will make you wish you'd never been born. I've seen what he does to people who cross him and it's not pretty."

"Who the hell are you?"

"Your worst nightmare."

The thug laughed. Leigh's heart leapt into a wild staccato. The man had his left arm locked around her waist. His right held the gun against her temple. She could hear the rush of his ragged breath in her ear. She could smell the fear coming off him to mingle with her own.

"Let her go and I'll let you walk away," Jake said. "I have no quarrel with you."

"Walk away from a big payoff?" The thug traced the gun down the side of her face. "I don't think you want to mess up this pretty face any more than I do."

"Or maybe this is a losing proposition for both of us," Jake said, edging closer.

They reached the elevator. The thug loosened his grip on her to press the down button. The gun wavered. Knowing this could be her only chance, that she had only an instant to act, Leigh grasped his gun wrist with both hands. Simultaneously, she brought her boot down on his instep.

The weapon exploded inches from her ear. The thug jerked the gun in Jake's direction. In her peripheral vision she saw Jake charge, his weapon leveled on the thug.

"No!" she screamed.

Jake took down the thug in a flying tackle. They hit the floor and rolled in a tangle of arms and legs. Hands grappled for guns.

A second gunshot blew a hole in the wall. Jake's hand circled the thug's wrist, but the other man's finger was on the trigger.

Run.

The word echoed inside her head, a primal instinct born of six years of living on the edge. But Leigh didn't run. Even though she knew Jake was more than capable of taking care of himself, there was no way she could leave him struggling with an armed killer twice his size.

Not giving herself time to debate, she bent and slid the knife from her boot. Gripping the dull side of the blade in a five-finger grip, she waited for a clean shot. She drew back and let the weapon fly in a short range, half spin throw, exactly the way they'd taught her at the knife-throwing classes she'd taken two years ago.

The knife spun as if in slow motion, the blade glinting in a perfect downward arc. An instant later the razor sharp point found its mark at the back of the man's left calf and went in deep.

The thug's body went rigid. An animalistic bellow tore from this throat. He turned murderous eyes on her. "You *bitch!*"

Jake grabbed the man's wrist, and the gun flew from his grip and skittered away. "That's no way to speak to a lady."

But the thug was more focused on the knife sticking out of his calf than he was on fighting. His features were contorted in pain. "I'm bleeding! She stabbed me!"

"You had it coming." Jake pulled a set of cuffs from his belt and secured the man's hands behind his back.

Leigh saw blood coming through his trousers, and for the first time it struck her what she'd done. She'd never hurt another human being in her life. Even though she hadn't had a choice, the realization made her feel a little sick. The room dipped and began to spin.

"Leigh."

She looked up to see Jake striding toward her, his expression taut. "Easy," he said. "Don't look at it."

She barely heard him over the rapid-fire beat of her heart. She could hear her breaths coming short and fast, her arms and legs trembling violently. Shock, she thought dully and was surprised, because she'd always thought she was tougher than that.

"I'm okay," she heard herself say.

"You're going to be real sorry you cut me," the thug snarled, his face twisted in rage and pain.

When Jake reached her, Leigh couldn't find her voice. All she could think was that they'd had a very close brush with death.

She jolted when Jake's hands closed around her arms and squeezed them. "It's okay," he said.

"I stabbed him."

"You saved my life. He didn't give you a choice."

Intellectually Leigh knew he was right. But on a more emotional level, nothing had felt right about sinking a knife into a man's flesh. Even if the man had had it coming.

"Where did you learn to throw a knife like that?"

"I...took a class. A couple of years ago."

"Must have been one hell of a class." He was running his hands up and down her arms. Talking to her. Trying to bring her back from the brink of shock.

Both of them jumped when the elevator chimed. Jake spun. As if in slow motion she saw him slide the gun from its sheath. With his other hand, he took hers.

"Run!" he shouted.

The next thing she knew she was being dragged down the hall toward the stairwell. But it was the sight of the two men stepping off the elevator that snapped her back to reality. At first glance she thought they were deputy marshals from the Witness Security Program. Then she noticed their guns and knew the situation was about to take a hard turn for the worse.

The first shot snapped through the air with the violence of a lightning strike. Sheetrock exploded off the wall two feet to her right. A hot *whiz* ignited the air just inches from her ear.

Thunk! Thunk! Thunk!

The stairwell at the end of the hall seemed a mile away. There was no cover. No place to run. All Leigh could think was that they were sitting ducks.

"I said run, damn it!"

She looked over at Jake and saw fear in his eyes, felt that same fear rampaging through her. She didn't think they were going to get out of this alive.

Then she caught a glimpse of red coming through his coat. *Blood,* she thought, and the fear ratcheted into terror. "Jake! Oh my God! You've been hit!"

The only response she got was the frenzied pound of her heart.

Chapter Three

"If I go down, you keep running!" Jake shouted. "You got that?"

"Don't go down," she panted.

He gave her a look and cursed. Leigh figured he already knew she wasn't the kind of person who left someone behind. Even if she didn't necessarily like that someone.

Shifting the gun, Jake took aim and shot out two wall sconces, throwing them into darkness. Cover, Leigh thought, and a sliver of relief went through her. At least they were no longer sitting ducks.

Shouts and heavy footsteps sounded behind them. White flashes exploded as gunfire erupted. Leigh ran at a reckless speed. But Jake urged her to go faster. At some point he'd forced her ahead of him. Belatedly, she realized he was keeping himself squarely between her and the gunmen.

They reached the end of the hall. Jake hit the stairwell door with both hands. The door flew open and banged against the wall. They burst into the stairwell. There was just enough light for Leigh to see the pipe rail and concrete steps. She was halfway down the first flight when she realized Jake wasn't beside her. She stopped and looked up to see him put his fist through the firefighter emergency box mounted on the wall. Glass exploded. She saw blood on his knuckles.

"What are you doing?" she asked.

"Taking out a little insurance." He yanked the coiled hose from its nest. "Go! I'll catch up."

She managed a few more steps before stopping. She looked back to see Jake ram the steel nozzle of the firefighter hose through the door handle and secure the other end to the stair rail, effectively locking out the men. He quickly tied off the hose. Banging sounded on the other side of the door, followed by gunshots. "That ought to buy us a couple of seconds," he muttered dryly and took the steps to her two at a time.

"Let's hope there's not a welcoming committee waiting for us outside."

He met her on the landing. "I told you to keep moving."

"I don't take orders from you."

The next thing she knew her hand was in his and she was barreling down the stairs, taking two and three steps at a time, certain she was going to fall at any second.

When they reached the ground level, Jake darted to the stairwell door and shoved it open. Winter rain greeted them with a cold, wet slap.

"My car's on the other side of the parking lot," Leigh said.

Heavy footsteps sounded from the stairwell above. Rasmussen's thugs had broken through.

"We'll take mine," Jake said. "Let's go."

They sprinted across the parking lot to an SUV the size of a tank. Jake punched the remote. "Climb in and hit the deck."

Leigh ran to the passenger side door, yanked it open. Jake was already behind the wheel, turning the key, shifting into gear. "Get down."

She glanced toward the motel in time to see two men burst from the door she and Jake had just exited. She heard shouts. Several muffled pops sounded.

"They're shooting at us!" she said.

Jake shoved her head down. "Stay the hell down!"

Then the SUV shot forward like a racecar out of pit row. A volley of shots splintered the air. Jake yanked the wheel hard to the left. A bullet blew a hole through the windshield. Glass rained down on Leigh. She peeked up to see tiny white cracks spreading like a network of capillaries across the windshield.

"Hang on!" Jake hit the gas. "This is going to be rough."

The SUV jumped the curb, bouncing wildly over a hedgerow and flowerbed. He twisted the steering wheel, but he wasn't fast enough to avoid the Dumpster, which screeched across concrete. Cursing, Jake swung the vehicle around and headed toward the street.

An abrupt and uneasy silence ensued, the

only sounds coming from the hum of the engine and the hiss of tires against wet pavement. Nausea churned in her stomach and for an uncomfortable moment she feared she would be sick.

"Are you all right?"

Trembling, Leigh sat up. "I feel like I have to throw up."

Jake glanced at her, his eyes dark with concern. "I can't pull over."

Feeling sweat break out on her forehead, she rolled down the window a few inches and let the cold air rush over her heated skin.

"Take some deep breaths," he said.

She did, and slowly the nausea receded. In its wake, she was hit by the wrenching knowledge that they'd come very close to being killed. That a monster was out of its cage. That he was a predator and she was his prey, and he wouldn't stop until he killed her. Then she remembered the blood on Jake's coat and her focus shifted.

"How bad are you hit?"

"Just a nick."

A shudder of relief went through her. "How

can Rasmussen be so organized and have so much power after six years in prison?"

"He's had a lot of contact with the outside. Lawyers. Accountants. He's got money stashed in overseas banks. He's connected. He's brutal. There aren't many people willing to cross him." Jake grimaced. "You crossed him."

"So did you."

His jaw flexed. "Yeah, well, he's not obsessed with me."

She looked down and saw that her hands were shaking. She hated being afraid, hated having to look over her shoulder. She'd spent the past six years rebuilding her life. A new name. A new job. A new apartment. Now, just when she'd finally found some semblance of normalcy and a life she was content with, the nightmare was starting all over again.

"Where are we going?"

"For now we're just putting some distance between us and those sons of bitches with guns."

Feeling sick again, she put her face in her hands. Hot tears burned behind her lids, but Leigh had grown adept at keeping a handle on her emotions. What she couldn't control was the fear. She was so tired of feeling like a victim.

After a moment she drew a deep breath and looked at Jake. Her gaze went to the hole in his coat. Right side, just above his hip. It was the size of a quarter. The surrounding material was blood soaked.

"Oh, Jake, you're bleeding."

"I can drive."

"That's more than just a nick. It looks bad. You need to—"

"We can't stop, Leigh."

"Can you call someone at the agency for help? Have them meet us somewhere? Get you some medical attention?"

Jake didn't answer, but she saw his hands tighten on the wheel, and something else began to niggle at her. It surprised her that even after so many years, she still knew him so well. They'd spent one short week together a lifetime ago. But it had been a week of life-and-death danger, of breathless intensity and a roller-coaster ride of emotions. They'd had a common goal, had been fighting a common monster. And for a precious moment in time, they'd shared the same reckless passions....

Leigh pushed those memories away. "Don't you have to call in to the agency and let them know what happened?"

Jake glanced at her, the rearview mirror and then back to the road ahead. "No."

"What do you mean no?"

"I mean I walked away from the agency this morning."

Leigh didn't know what to say. For Jake it had always been about the job. About getting his man, no holds barred. He defined himself by his work. Six years ago he'd been willing to sacrifice her to get at Rasmussen. Something she'd never been able to forgive him for.

She knew all too well how much his job with the MIDNIGHT Agency meant to him. She couldn't help but wonder why he would walk away. She told herself it didn't matter. Nothing he did now was going to change what had happened six years ago. But then, she'd always been good at lying to herself when it came to Jake.

"I hope your leaving the agency didn't have anything to do with me," she said.

"If I hadn't walked away this morning, you'd be lying stone-cold dead back at that motel." He shot her a dark look. "Or else on your way to Rasmussen."

"You don't know that."

His laugh told her he did. "You might think you can handle this on your own, Leigh, but I'm telling you, you can't. I'm asking you not to try."

"I'm not the same dumb kid I was when I met you, Jake."

"I never thought you were a dumb kid."

"You just treated me like one. Until it came time for you to get what you needed, anyway." Leigh shivered as the memory of that day pressed into her. The MIDNIGHT Agency had wired her for sound. She'd met with Rasmussen at his Michigan Avenue loft. It had been the worst day of her life. But she'd gotten Rasmussen to incriminate himself on tape. Only, she'd had to sell her soul to do it....

Shaking off the memory, she sighed. "Look, I know how to disappear. All I need is a new name. A new city—"

"He's not going to stop looking for you," Jake interrupted. "How long do you think you can hide? A week? A month? A year? Sooner or later your number is going to come up."

"He's a fugitive. He can't elude the police indefinitely."

"If he flees the country, it could be years before we get him. He's got the resources to stay hidden as long as it takes."

"As long as it takes for what?" As soon as the words were out she regretted them, because she knew what he was going to say.

"To find you," he said tightly. "I don't even want to think about what he'll do to you. Damn it, you know him, Leigh. He's obsessed with you. He's bent on revenge. Motivated by jealousy and hate and ego. You saw the way he looked at you in court the day you testified against him. He's fixated on you. He knows what happened—" He bit off the words and looked away. "Between us."

Even with her heart pounding with fear, she felt an unwelcome surge of heat at the mention of what had happened between her and Jake six years ago. Leigh knew it was crazy, but that was the way it had been between them. Even with their lives on the line, they hadn't been able to resist each other. A single, earth-shattering night in his arms and she'd been lost....

"How could I have been so naive to get involved with a man like Ian Rasmussen?" she whispered.

Jake rolled his shoulder. "You couldn't have known what kind of man he was. He kept his secrets well hidden. He was Chicago's favorite bad-boy bachelor. He had a successful North Michigan Avenue restaurant. The local media loved him."

"I was with him for almost a year."

"Don't start the blame game, Leigh. You were young. Inexperienced. He knew that and used those things to manipulate you."

Even after all this time, it made her feel like a fool. Yes, she'd been young—just twenty-one when she met Ian Rasmussen. But why had it taken so long for her to see him for what he really was?

As if realizing where her thoughts had gone, Jake turned to her. "If it hadn't been for you, he never would have gone to trial."

The mention of the trial made her feel queasy. The court proceedings had been a nightmare. Leigh had taken the stand to testify against Rasmussen. Only, Rasmussen's high-powered lawyer had done his best to put her and the MIDNIGHT Agency on trial instead. That was when it had come out that she and Jake had been intimate. That the MIDNIGHT Agency had formally disciplined Jake for inappropriate conduct with a witness. Rasmussen's lawyer had tried to use the information to get the case thrown out. The judge however had seen through the ruse. But Rasmussen had gone off the deep end. Not only had Leigh betrayed him by wearing a wire and getting him on tape for the feds, but she'd betrayed him on an even deeper level by sleeping with the very man who'd brought him down.

For a second, when she looked across the seat at Jake, she saw him as the man he'd been six years ago. He'd been her protector, heat and strength and steel control. But Leigh had seen that control fracture. She would never forget the way he'd looked at her the first time he'd kissed her. The way his eyes had gone dark when he'd touched her. She would never forget the way he'd trembled when he'd been inside her. Or the moment when her own control had shattered with a power that had moved her to tears....

Like it or not, those images were forever branded on her heart.

"He's never going to stop looking for me, is he?" she asked after a moment.

Jake's dark expression said it all. "No," he murmured.

Chapter Four

Jake didn't think the bullet had hit anything vital, but it hurt like a son of a bitch. By late afternoon he'd accepted the fact that he wasn't going to make it to his destination, a small town in Michigan. A place where he had friends and family and a safe place to stash Leigh until Rasmussen was caught.

So much for best-laid plans.

The wound throbbed with every beat of his heart. He could feel his clothes sticking to his skin where the blood had dried. The pain was making him sweat, making him cranky. He was going to have to find a place to pull over and check the damage. The question was where. They were in the middle of farm country, somewhere in eastern Kansas, surrounded by fields and prairie grasses.

"Jake, you're still bleeding. We're going to have to stop."

He glanced at Leigh and even though he was hurting and annoyed, her beauty took him aback. He could see how a man could become obsessed with her. She was innocence and sin rolled into a single, stunning package. But his attraction to her went far deeper than her physical beauty. He'd been drawn to the goodness of her soul, to the kindness in her heart that had spoken to his on a level he couldn't begin to explain.

"I know," he said. "Not yet."

"I'm not going to sit here and let you pass out."

"I'm not going to pass out, damn it."

But now that she'd mentioned it, he knew she was right. Jake glanced down at the hole in his coat. His stomach fluttered uneasily at the sight of fresh blood. It had soaked his coat and was now dripping onto the seat. Damn. Damn. *Damn!*

"You don't want to let a bullet wound go untreated," she persisted. "Even if it's minor."

"I know what I need to do," he snapped. "Get off my back."

Just west of the Missouri State line, he turned onto a county road and pulled over. He couldn't hide the wince of pain when he shifted to ease the cell phone from his belt.

Leigh looked at him, her expression worried. "Do you want me to drive?"

"I just need to make a call."

He punched the only number he could think of. Mike Madrid was not only a highly trained MIDNIGHT agent but a good friend. Madrid answered on the second ring with a curt utterance of his name.

"This isn't a secure line," Jake said.

A pause. "I hope you know you screwed up when you walked out of there this morning."

"Not the first time."

"Could be your last if you don't make nice with Cutter."

"Look, I have the package, but I got sacked."

Mike Madrid swore. *Sacked* was code for *shot*. "How bad?"

"Minor. But I need an Auntie Em." A place to stay in Kansas.

"I'll send you a card." Code for a text message on Jake's Blackberry.

"Roger."

Jake disconnected.

"I didn't get all of that," Leigh said.

"Neither did anyone else." He started to reach for the Blackberry in the back seat, but the movement caused a tearing sensation in the wound, wrenching a groan from him.

"Jake, we've got to get you to a doctor."

"Hand me the Blackberry out of that leather bag, will you?"

Shaking her head, Leigh reached into the bag and withdrew the tiny wireless handheld computer. He tried to take it from her, but she stopped him. "Stop acting like a macho jerk and let me do it for you."

Shoving back his annoyance, partly because she was right, Jake leaned against the seat. "Hit the power button. Wait for it to boot. Hit Receive."

He watched her hit the tiny buttons, liking the way her brows knit, the way she bit her lip in concentration. They'd put three hundred miles between them and Rasmussen's men. But Jake knew it wasn't enough. It would never be enough. Rasmussen would never stop looking for her. Watching her,

Jake vowed he would do whatever it took to keep Rasmussen from hurting her.

"It's a map," she said after a moment.

Jake reached for the Blackberry and squinted at the tiny screen. "There's a place we can go to rest about fifty miles north of here."

"Jake, I don't think you can make it that far."

"I don't have a choice."

THEY DROVE PAST a huge road sign welcoming them to the great state of Missouri. Quaint farmhouses with silos and big red barns dotted the countryside. The sky had been overcast throughout the day. But as the sun sank in the west, dark clouds began to roil on the northern horizon, and Jake knew it was too cold for rain.

The first flakes of snow swirled as he turned the Hummer onto the gravel lane. In the distance, an old two-story farmhouse rose out of the flat ground like a jut of rock. As they drew nearer, he could see that the house was in rough shape. Paint that had once been white was weathered gray by years of neglect, and the harsh elements of the Midwestern seasons. Two ramshackle barns were just a gust of wind away from falling down. The house was surrounded by two hundred acres of vacant farmland.

The place was desolate and in the open. If anyone came for them, Jake would be able to see them coming. But he didn't think anyone would find them here. For a few hours they would be safe. Once they rested and he got his wound cleaned up, he could decide what to do next.

"I hope you made reservations," Leigh said.

All Jake could think was that he wished they were going to the kind of place that required reservations. The kind of place where they could sip champagne in front of a roaring fire. The kind of place with a king-size bed and linen sheets. A place where he could lay her down and peel away her clothes layer by layer until she was naked and trembling beneath him....

Jake parked the Hummer at the rear of the house and shut off the engine. The snow was coming down in earnest, the weatherman calling for several inches before morning. As long as it didn't get any worse than that, he supposed they would be all right here.

A brutal north wind hit him like a bucket of ice water when he opened the door. Knowing he would be stiff, he cautiously slid from the truck. Without warning, his leg buckled. Grimacing, he dropped to his knees.

"Jake!"

Leigh rounded the front of the vehicle and knelt beside him. "My God! What happened?"

"I'm fine, damn it." Embarrassment roughened his voice.

"Oh, I can see you're fine."

"My leg stiffened up on me, that's all." But for an uncomfortable moment he wasn't sure if he could make it to his feet. And he began to wonder if the bullet wound was worse than he'd assumed. Whenever he put weight on the leg, the pain clamped down on him like a fanged beast.

"Let me help you."

He was about to snap at her, but when he looked into her eyes and saw her concern, the words died in his throat. For the first time he noticed that her hands were on his shoulders. He knew it was stupid, considering the circumstances, but he liked having her touch him. It reminded him of the way it had felt when she'd touched him six years ago. It was the kind of touching a man never forgot.

"I can do it." Shrugging off her hands, he used the door to pull himself to his feet.

"Are there any supplies inside? Running water? Blankets?"

He motioned toward the rear of the Hummer. "There's a first-aid kit in the back. A blanket, too. Bring them in. I'm going to clear the house."

Jake limped to the porch at the rear of the house and crossed to the door. He wasn't surprised to find the door locked. Looking around, he spied a hand shovel and used it to break the pane of glass next to the knob. Reaching inside, he twisted the bolt lock and opened the door.

He noticed that the kitchen wasn't much warmer than outside, aside from being protected from the wind. The counters were 1970s yellow Formica and covered with a thick later of dust. The white porcelain sink was chipped. The linoleum was badly scuffed and curling in the corners. He crossed to the sink, twisted the faucet, and water burst from the tap. At least they had water.

He limped to the living room. The tall windows were grimy and draped with gauzy curtains, letting in little light. But it didn't take much light to see that the place had long since fallen to disrepair. Still, Jake was grateful to have a roof over his head.

The high ceilings were water stained. In some places the plaster had chipped away and fallen to the floor. A fireplace constructed of crumbling brick dominated the room. An antique potbellied stove sat in the corner. The only piece of furniture was a table that looked as if it had been used for a workbench.

Not the Ritz-Carlton, but it was going to have to do.

Moving to the front door, Jake opened it and looked out at the porch. Relief swept through him when he spotted the firewood stacked haphazardly. If they burned wood conservatively, it might get them through the night.

Not wanting to think of spending the night with Leigh in a cold farmhouse, he limped to the woodpile and gathered as much as he could carry into his arms. He locked the door behind him and went over to the hearth. A surge of light-headedness hit him when he saw Leigh standing in the kitchen doorway. He wasn't sure if it was from the bullet wound or the effect she always had on him, but it was enough to make him break into a sweat.

"I'll make a fire," he said.

Quickly she set the first-aid kit and blanket on the table and came to him. "Let me help you."

He didn't want her help. He didn't like the way he was reacting to her. But the pain was wearing down his bravado. He let her take some of the firewood from his arms.

"Are you sure we weren't followed?" she asked.

"I'm sure."

"How long will we stay?"

"Long enough to get my wound cleaned up and grab a couple of hours of sleep."

"Then what?"

He put a match to the newspaper he'd set

under the wood and watched it burst into flames. "Hopefully Rasmussen will be in custody by then."

"And if he isn't?"

He looked at her and felt another surge of light-headedness. "We cross that path when we come to it."

Jake rose and carried some wood to the potbellied stove. When both the fireplace and stove were blazing, he walked to the kitchen where Leigh had set out the first-aid kit.

"Nice kit," she said.

"Courtesy of the MIDNIGHT Agency," he said.

She opened the lid and picked up a wrapped syringe. "Looks like they thought of everything."

"Yeah, I think Cutter used to be a Boy Scout."

Her smile was short-lived. "I'm sorry you left the agency on bad terms. I know how much your career means to you."

Jake said nothing.

"Was it because of me?"

"It was because of a difference of opinion between Sean Cutter and me. It's not the first time."

"Will you be able to go back?"

Jake sighed, the gravity of what he had done this morning weighing him down. "I don't think he'll ask me to come back."

Not wanting to deal with that at the moment, he looked down to where the blood was still seeping through his coat. "Are you up to handling this bullet wound?"

"I was ready hours ago." But he didn't miss the flicker of uncertainty in her eyes. She motioned toward the table. "Why don't you take off your coat and have a seat?"

Jake worked the coat off his shoulders. He tugged his shirt from the waistband and was dismayed to see so much blood. The bullet had gone though his coat, through his blue jeans and grazed his right hip, close to the muscular part of the buttock. Terrific. He pondered the dilemma, but there was no way around it. He was going to have to remove his pants.

"I hate to do this to you, Leigh, but I'm going to have to lose the pants."

She looked more horrified by the idea of seeing his bare butt than she did at the prospect of treating a potentially serious bullet wound. But she quickly regained her composure. "It won't be the first time I've seen you without them."

Her cheeks were flushed. Jake could feel that same heat creeping up his own cheeks. And other parts of his body he didn't want to think about.

Without looking at her, he unsnapped his jeans, tugged them down and stepped out of them. He wore plain white boxer briefs. He glanced at the blood-soaked material. "Going to need a new wardrobe after this," he muttered. "Bullet put a hole in everything but my shoes."

Leigh was looking everywhere but into his eyes. Jake wasn't shy, but he didn't like the idea of dropping his pants in front of a woman he'd spent the past six years trying to get out of his system. One stray thought, and his body might just react in a way he didn't want it to. Something like that was hard to hide when you were half naked.

Because he needed something to do, he reached into the first-aid kit and picked up the syringe. "Think you can get some antibiot-ics into me?"

"I have a feeling you're not talking about a pill."

He smiled as he tore the wrapper from the syringe. "Penicillin. Intramuscular injection. Needs to go in the hip." He patted his left hip. "Alcohol swabs are in the kit."

"Jake, I've never given a shot before."

"You'll do fine. Find the muscle. Jab the needle straight in." He demonstrated. "De-press the plunger. Out quickly." He handed her the syringe.

"What if I hurt you?"

"It won't be the first time."

He hadn't meant to say that. In the last hours he hadn't meant for a lot of things to happen.

She started to turn away, but he reached out and touched her arm. A small thrill raced through him when her gaze met his. "I'm a big guy," he said. "That's a small needle. You're not going to hurt me." When she hes-itated, he frowned. "What will hurt me is if I pick up an infection from that damn bullet." Bracing himself against the table with one hand, he used the other to pull down one side of his boxers. "Ready?"

Chapter Five

Leigh had never been squeamish, but her hands were shaking as she scrubbed a small area with alcohol, set her hand against his hip and took aim with the needle. His flesh was warm and granite hard beneath her palm. Even though the moment was not sexual in any way, she found herself remembering what it had been like to touch him intimately. Six years ago she hadn't been able to get enough of him....

Suppressing her memories with the proficiency of a woman who did it often, she steadied herself and jabbed the needle into the muscle. Jake didn't so much as wince when she depressed the plunger then quickly withdrew the needle.

"That wasn't so bad, was it?" Tugging up

his briefs, he took the syringe from her and dropped it into a biohazard bag. ·

"In the scope of things, administering that injection doesn't even make the scale of difficult. I think the real problem we're facing here is figuring out what to do next," she said.

"I've got a safe place for you to stay until Rasmussen is caught."

"Or maybe you want to use me as bait. You know, win my trust and then send me back into the lion's den to see if he'll bite."

Leigh knew it had been an unreasonable thing to say. She hadn't meant to dredge up the past. But she was tired and stressed out. Worse, she was still angry with Jake for the way things had ended six years ago. For making her feel something for him when he'd known nothing could ever come of it. For putting her in an impossible situation where she'd had no choice but to compromise herself. For not stopping her when he could have.

"I didn't send you to Rasmussen," Jake snapped. "You did that all by yourself."

"You knew there was no other way. Just as you knew I'd go through with it."

"Leigh, after everything that happened between us I never would have put you in that position. I don't share, damn it."

"You did, Jake."

Lowering his head, he pinched the bridge of his nose and sighed. "Leigh, I can't undo what's already been done. If I could, I would. All I can do now is try to keep you safe."

"Then you'll forgive me if I don't trust your motives." Using another alcohol wipe, Leigh disinfected her hands, hating that they were shaking. Hating even more that her emotions were jumbled and conflicting. Anger and the old hurt warred with an attraction that had not diminished in the years since she'd last seen him.

If it were anyone but Jake standing before her in nothing but his boxers, this wouldn't be so difficult. But seeing him hurt and bleeding and half-naked made her remember things she didn't want to remember. Made her feel things she didn't want to feel.

Jake braced one hand against the table and used the other to tug down one side of his briefs. Leigh's stomach did a slow roll as she took in the sight of the wound. It was a deep graze. The bullet had dug a three-inch gash through the flesh. The surrounding skin was the color of an overripe plum, swollen and hot to the touch.

"Oh God, Jake, it's bad. You've lost a lot of blood. No wonder you're in pain."

He turned his head and studied the wound. "If it was bad, I wouldn't be standing." But Leigh didn't miss the way his face went pale.

"There's some butterfly tape in the kit," he said. "Clean it up, use the tape to close the wound, and bandage it."

"You need to see a doctor."

"That's not an option."

A chill passed through her when she looked out the window and realized night had fallen. The wind was keening around the old house, like a ghost looking for shelter from the cold. She hated being afraid, jumping at shadows. Hated even more knowing Rasmussen was out there, using every resource he had to find her.

"What if he finds us here, Jake?"

"He won't." But there was little conviction in his voice.

Leigh did her best not to cause him pain

as she disinfected the wound and applied the butterfly tape to close it. But she could tell by the way his muscles tensed that she was hurting him.

By the time she finished the bandage, she was trembling with tension. "Have you got something for the pain?" she asked.

"Acetaminophen in the kit." He winced as he grabbed his pants.

Leigh handed him the blanket. "Let me wash the blood from your clothes."

Jake looked as if he wanted to protest, but he took the blanket and wrapped it around his hips. "I'll do it. Just get me the pills."

Securing the blanket at his hips, he worked off his boxers and took both his jeans and shorts to the sink. Leigh met him there a moment later with three Tylenol in her hand.

He downed them dry and proceeded to scrub the blood from his boxers. Without asking, Leigh picked up his jeans and used an old bar of soap to scrub the blood from the fabric.

"So what do we do now?" she asked.

"Try to get some rest. We've got running

water. Heat. I think I've got a couple of protein bars in the Hummer. We leave at first light."

"To where?"

He said nothing.

"Your place?"

"I didn't get to be a federal agent by being stupid, Leigh."

"That would certainly draw Rasmussen out, wouldn't it?"

He shot her a dark look. "You're going to have to trust me."

"The last time I trusted you it cost me—" Shocked by what she'd almost said, Leigh bit off the words.

Jake stared hard at her, his eyes digging into her, seeking answers she didn't want to give. "You never told me, Leigh. What exactly did you have to do to get the goods on Rasmussen six years ago?"

Struggling against the shame and anguish threatening to overwhelm her, she stared back at him. "You should know, Jake. But then I was expendable, wasn't I?"

As realization dawned, fury flashed in the dark depths of his eyes. But it was not directed at her. And suddenly it hit her that he hadn't known.

Taking the jeans from her, he turned away and walked to the living room without responding. Pressing her hand to her stomach, Leigh remained in the kitchen. What had just happened? Was Jake angry with Ian Rasmussen? With her? Or was he angry with himself?

When she'd calmed down, she followed. He was in the process of draping the jeans and briefs over the hot potbellied stove. "Should be dry in a couple of hours," he said.

"How does the wound feel?"

"Going to be stiff for a couple of days." His voice was milder, but still he didn't look at her. "I'll have a nice scar to add to my collection."

The image of his battle-scarred body came to her in a vivid flash. She'd felt his hard muscles flex beneath her hands. She'd sensed the power within him, and she'd seen that power unleashed.

That she could remember with such startling clarity made her realize she was going to have to be careful in the coming days. Jake Vanderpol was a dynamic man, especially when he wanted something.

Leigh wondered if he wanted something from her. If that something had to do with getting Rasmussen. Or if it was much more personal.

LEIGH UNCOVERED an old cast-iron pot in one of the kitchen cabinets and heated water on the stove. An hour later and six trips up the creaky old stairs, and the old claw-foot tub in the upstairs bathroom was almost full. She found a candle and set it on a broken plate and carried it upstairs.

Looking down into the steaming water, she had never wanted a bath as badly as she did right now. Quickly she stripped off her clothes and sank into the hot water all the way up to her chin. It was a small pleasure, but one she wouldn't trade for anything.

She hadn't spoken to Jake since their exchange earlier. He seemed restless and brooding, and Leigh would just as soon not deal with him when her own emotions were strung tight. He'd walked to the Hummer and retrieved two protein bars. They'd eaten in silence. He hadn't spoken of Rasmussen. But Leigh had seen him watching her.

She lay back in the hot water trying to shut out all thoughts of him. But Jake Vanderpol was not the kind of man a woman could easily erase from her mind. She'd been trying to forget him for six years. Even with all the unresolved issues between them, something had remained. Something that could not be shaken by time or absence or even the hurt he had caused her.

She jolted when her cell phone rang. Sitting up, she looked around and in the candlelight located her cell phone on the floor next to her bra and panties. Who would be calling her? The people from the Witness Security Program? Had Ian Rasmussen been caught? Was she safe? Could she go home?

Bolstered by those hopes, she reached for the phone. The number on the display wasn't familiar. She hit the talk button. "Hello?"

"Don't hang up."

The refined voice, the words spoken so softly, made her heart beat madly, and the water suddenly felt ice cold. "Ian. Wh-what are you doing?"

"I'm trying to stay alive, Leigh. There are men out there who want to kill me. They think I'm a criminal."

"You are a criminal. You need to turn yourself in."

"Prison is no place for a man like me. But then, you knew it would be hard for me, didn't you? And yet you did what you had to do to put me away anyway, didn't you?"

"You were going to kill me."

"I loved you, Leigh. I would never hurt you. You know that."

"Ian, you need to turn yourself in." It was the only thing she could think of to say.

"You and I have some unfinished business, Leigh. You and I and Jake Vanderpol."

Her heart beat even faster. "I have no business with you."

"You've been with him, haven't you? I hear it in your voice. You've given him your body."

His tone changed then. Refined, yet with something ugly and menacing just beneath the surface. "I'm going to make him pay when I get my hands on him, Leigh. I can promise you you'll hear every second of what I do to him."

"Don't." The single word was all she could manage. Leigh had never considered herself weak. She had certainly never considered herself a coward. In the year she'd been with Ian Rasmussen, he'd never so much as laid a hand on her. But she feared him like she'd never feared another human being in her life.

"I miss you, Leigh."

A sound escaped her when the bathroom door swung open. For a terrible moment she envisioned Rasmussen bursting into the room. Jake dead downstairs. Their fates sealed...

Then she saw Jake. Apprehension and grim determination showed on his face as he came over to the tub. In the candlelight she could see his eyes flicking from her to the phone in her hand. He must have seen something in her expression because he reached for the phone without speaking. "Who is this?" he said in a rough voice.

JAKE HAD HEARD the chirp of her cell phone through the heating vents and rushed upstairs.

If the caller was one of Leigh's friends, Rasmussen wouldn't hesitate to use them to glean their location. The arms dealer wasn't above torture when it came to getting what he wanted.

Steam hovered like wet ghosts when he burst through the door. In the back of his mind it occurred to him she was taking a bath, that he probably wasn't welcome. He caught a glimpse of her skin glistening in the soft light. But all sexual thoughts vanished when he saw her face, and *knew* who the caller was.

Taking the phone from her, he put it to his ear and turned away to give her privacy. "Who is this?"

"Judging from your tone, I think you know. How are you, Mr. Vanderpol?"

"I can have this call traced," Jake said. "Triangulation and we'll have you within the hour."

"Why don't you do that?"

Jake said nothing. He knew better than to let a scumbag like Rasmussen get to him, but he wanted to take the other man down so badly he could taste it.

"That's what I thought," Rasmussen said.

"What the hell do you want?"

"Leigh, of course. Your death will be a bonus."

Jake forced a laugh. "Why don't you do yourself a favor and turn yourself in? Give me a location and I'll have an agent pick you up. You can resolve this peaceably."

"Peaceably is hardly my style."

"Any other way and you won't survive."

The pause that followed was so long that for a moment, Jake thought Rasmussen had disconnected. Then Rasmussen lowered his voice and said, "Have you been with her yet?"

"I don't know what you're talking about." But Jake knew exactly what the bastard was talking about, and he hated it. "I think you're one twisted son of a bitch."

"Ah, a gentleman. You don't kiss and tell, do you, Vanderpol?" A harsh laugh sounded. "Was she worth it?"

"Worth what?"

"Giving it all up for?"

Jake couldn't respond. All he could do was stand there and wonder how Rasmussen knew about his leaving the agency. "Turn yourself in, Rasmussen."

"Enjoy her while you can, Vanderpol." His voice intensified. "Because I'm coming for her. I'm going to take her from you. And I'm going to make you beg for—"

Jake disconnected. Even though the room was cold, sweat had broken out on the back of his neck.

How the hell had Rasmussen known about his leaving the agency just that morning?

"Jake?"

Her voice pulled him back, but he didn't turn to face her. For the first time he noticed the candlelight. That the bathroom smelled like her. A sweet, earthy scent that titillated his senses, made him long for something that had eluded him for what seemed like forever.

"Don't answer your phone again," he said.

"I didn't know it was him."

He turned to face her. "Cell phones can be traced."

"I didn't know," she said.

The candle didn't throw off much light, but it was enough for him to see the loveliness of her face. Jake swore he wasn't going to look at the rest of her. But his eyes betrayed him and skimmed over the enticing curve of her shoulders. The graceful length of her throat. The old porcelain tub was tall, and he was standing far enough away that it covered the rest of her. But he had seen her naked. He had had the image of her smooth, silky skin branded in his brain.

Remembering the nights they'd spent holed up in a safe house, he went hard. His head began to whirl as all the blood in his body rushed south. For several interminable minutes he just stood there, need pulsing through his body.

She stared back at him, her mouth partially open as if in surprise. All he could think of were the times he'd kissed that mouth. All the times that mouth had been on his, on his body.

"Get dressed," he heard himself say.

And then he left the room.

Chapter Six

Ian Rasmussen had made the call via his satellite phone. "Did you get the trace?" he asked.

"We've located the nearest tower."

"Excellent. Where are they?"

"Western Missouri."

"Vanderpol drives a Hummer. That size vehicle shouldn't be hard to spot."

"The area is rural farmland. Snow is going to make it difficult. He could have parked it in an outbuilding or garage."

The slow burn of fury made Rasmussen's hands clench. He didn't want obstacles thrown in his path. He wanted action and he wanted it right now. "Do you know what I did to the last man who handed me excuses?"

The man on the other end of the line cleared his throat. "No, sir."

"I had him skinned alive and made gloves from his flesh."

Tense silence filled the line. "I understand," the man said.

"Good. Then you understand that all I care about is results. Are we on the same page?"

"Yes, sir."

"Find Jake Vanderpol. Find Leigh Michaels. Use every resource at your disposal. Call in every favor ever owed you. Money is not an option. I want both of them alive. And I want them *right now*."

"I'll do my best."

"You'd better hope your best is good enough," Rasmussen snapped, then disconnected.

LEIGH LAY ON HER SIDE a few feet from the potbellied stove listening to the wind whipping around the eaves and the snow hitting the windowpanes.

Even though her body ached with exhaustion, her mind was wound tight. Jake had given her the only blanket, but she was still freezing. He'd gotten up twice to put wood in both the stove and the fireplace. Evidently, she wasn't the only one with insomnia.

She wanted to believe it was fear eating away at her peace of mind and her ability to sleep. But she knew her wakefulness had little to do with Rasmussen and everything to do with the man sitting a few feet from the hearth, staring into the fire.

He hadn't spoken to her since the scene in the bathroom when Rasmussen had called. Leigh had wanted to talk, but something kept her from bridging the chasm that had fallen between them. Maybe it was because she didn't want to risk getting any closer to him.

She knew Jake was a good man. A good agent. It was the latter, though, that kept her from trusting him. Because while she knew he wanted to protect her, she also knew he was capable of sacrificing her to get his man. She had the scars on her heart to prove it.

"You're shivering."

She jolted at the sound of his voice. "It's cold," she said, sitting up.

He stood over her, looking down. Leigh wasn't sure why, but she felt edgy, ill at ease.

"How's the bullet wound?" she asked.

"Sore. Stiff." He smiled, and some of the tension leached from her neck and shoulders. "I'll live."

"Sounds like the snow is piling up."

"It's cold, Leigh. We need to get some sleep. I'm not sure when we'll be able to sleep again."

She knew what he was saying, what he was asking. He didn't ask for permission as he sat down beside her. She saw the intent in his eyes, but she didn't stop him when he put his arm around her and draped the blanket over both of them.

"Lie down with me," he said softly. "We'll stay a lot warmer together than we will alone."

The protest died on her lips when he eased her to the floor. It seemed only natural to rest her head against his shoulder. For the first time in too many months to count, Leigh felt safe—and oddly content. She felt that as long as she was with Jake, Ian Rasmussen and his band of thugs couldn't touch them, couldn't hurt them. Jake Vanderpol was a warrior. He was the most competent man Leigh had ever met.

That she could feel that way for him after what he'd done to her frightened her. Made her feel vulnerable. That once again she was making decisions based on her heart and not her brain.

"Better?" he asked after a moment.

"A lot better. Thank you."

She turned away so she was lying on her side, facing away from him. He cupped her body with his, solid and warm and so comforting she could feel all the fears and uncertainties draining away. He draped his arm over her in a protective gesture. But a new tension that was just as disconcerting rose in her body. Awareness crept over her. Her nerve endings sizzled where his body touched hers.

He shifted closer. Even though the movement wasn't sexual, she could feel her body responding to his closeness. Her breasts felt heavy and full. She felt a quivery sensation, need she didn't want to feel nipping at her.

Jake was only the second man she'd ever been with, and the experience had been breathtaking and intense, and Leigh had fallen hard and fast in love with him. She'd been just naive enough to believe he felt the same for her.

"You're still shaking," he whispered.

Leigh closed her eyes. "I'm still cold."

"I don't think that's why you're shaking." When she didn't answer, he put his hand on her shoulder and rolled her over so that they were lying face-to-face. "We need to talk about what happened last time," he said.

His eyes were dark in the firelight. But even in the semidarkness she could see the intensity burning there. My God, she thought, how could any woman not fall for this man?

"I'm sorry you got hurt," he said. "I know you think I used you, but I didn't."

"You got what you wanted." But she'd been so hurt that all she'd wanted to do was get away from Jake and the pain he'd caused her. She'd gone to his superiors with his plan, and they'd carried it out. Used her as a pawn.

And she'd paid a terrible price.

FOR SIX YEARS Jake had wondered what she'd had to do to get Rasmussen to confess on tape. His superiors at the MIDNIGHT Agency had sent her back to Rasmussen. She'd worn a wire into his North Michigan Avenue penthouse. And then she'd proceeded to glean information from him about a shipment of arms designated for delivery to a terrorist group. Because of Leigh, the MIDNIGHT Agency had been there waiting when Rasmussen and his men delivered the arms.

Jake's direct superior, Sean Cutter, had barred Jake from listening to the tapes that had been made of her encounter with Rasmussen, claiming he was too personally involved. But Jake had always suspected she'd had to sell a piece of her soul to save herself. The not knowing had eaten him alive for six unbearable years.

"That isn't the way it happened, Leigh. I don't use the people I care about."

"That's the way it felt."

Wanting her to believe him, hating the mistrust in her eyes, he set his hands on either side of her face. "You and I were together. Right or wrong, it happened. I don't sleep with someone with an agenda in mind. I sure as hell don't share them with a damn killer."

He could see tiny pinpoints of light in her eyes from the fire. She was so lovely. He hated that she thought he was capable of using her in such a terrible way. That she thought so little of him.

"Leigh, you've got to believe me. I never would have used you that way. I would have let Rasmussen go before I'd put you at risk like that."

"You put me in a terrible situation."

The need to pull her into his arms and crush her against him was overwhelming, but he didn't. He couldn't. Not when she believed he was capable of using her, putting her in harm's way.

"I didn't. Damn it, I would have found another way." The memory of the dark days after she'd gone into the Witness Security Program came back to him. "My superiors had no right to let you do it. If Rasmussen had figured out what you were doing, he would have killed you. When I found out what happened, I let them know what I thought about using a civilian the way they used you." The memory made him grimace. "I was disciplined and nearly lost my job. I wasn't scoring many points with the agency, and I think that was the beginning of the end of my career."

"I'm sorry that happened to you. Because of me."

"Because of Rasmussen. Not you."

"It looks like both of us paid a price."

For the first time, she looked at him as if she thought he might be telling the truth. As if she wanted to believe him. Forgive him.

It was all he needed. Jake's restraint broke with an audible snap. He pulled her against him. A groan escaped him when the softness of her body conformed to his. He'd been aroused off and on all evening, ever since seeing her in the tub. But now, holding her tightly, feeling her warmth, smelling the sweet scent of her skin, every nerve in his body jumped to attention.

A gasp escaped her when he shoved his hands through her hair. He marveled at the silky texture of it beneath his fingers. He could hear her breathing hard and knew she was every bit as affected as he was. He swore the room temperature went up fifty degrees.

Electricity arced between them when he touched his mouth to hers. It seemed like a lifetime since he'd tasted her, but kissing her now was worth every agonizing second of that wait. She made a halfhearted attempt to turn her head, but he redirected his aim and caught her mouth anyway. This time she gave it to him.

He hadn't planned on things going this far. He'd promised himself it would be enough just to convince her he hadn't used her. But once he'd touched her, once he'd kissed her, Jake couldn't stop. It had always been that way between them.

He should have known she would come to her senses.

Without warning, she pulled away and scrambled to her feet. For several interminable seconds they stared at each other. Then Jake sat up, scrubbed his hand over his jaw. "I'm sorry," he said. "I shouldn't have done that."

Leigh wouldn't look at him. She had the blanket wrapped around her, as if it would protect her from him, and looked everywhere but into his eyes. "You shouldn't have done a lot of things."

"At some point we're going to have to talk about what's between us," Jake said. "It's not going to go away."

Leigh wrapped her arms around herself as if from a sudden chill. "Fool me once, shame on you. Fool me twice, shame on me." She met his gaze. "I'm not going to let you hurt me again, Jake."

Before he could respond, she turned away and walked to the hearth, where she sat staring into the flames.

LEIGH WASN'T SURE what woke her. One moment she was lying on her side in a state of exhausted slumber. The next she was wide awake.

Sitting up, she pulled the blanket around her shoulders and looked around. In the dim light slanting in through the window she could see Jake. He was lying on his side a few feet from the potbellied stove. She could hear his rhythmic breathing, and the sound was soothing. The wood in the hearth had burned down to embers, and the room was so cold she could see her breath.

Being quiet so she wouldn't wake Jake, she got to her feet and padded to the woodpile he'd left at the door. If she couldn't sleep the least she could do was toss some fuel on the fire. She picked up two small logs and started toward the stove. Through the frosted glass of the window, she could see that the snow was still coming down.

Leigh gasped and nearly dropped the wood as a shadow flashed past the window. Her entire body trembling, she set the wood down and darted to Jake.

"Jake!" she whispered.

He was on his feet in an instant, his pistol in his hand. "What is it?"

"I saw someone outside the window."

He put his finger to his lips, then jogged silently to the window and looked out. "Put on your coat," he said and went to the kitchen.

Leigh did as she was told and waited, scared through and through. She sorely wished she hadn't left her pistol back at the motel.

Jake returned a few seconds later carrying a few supplies. "There are three of them in front of the house. We've got to go out the back."

"What about the Hummer?"

"Can't get to it." He jabbed his arms into his coat and put the supplies in the pockets. "Go. Now."

Leigh couldn't remember the last time she'd been so frightened. They were outnumbered and outgunned.

How had Rasmussen found them?

The next thing she knew, Jake had taken her arm and was shoving her into the kitchen and toward the back door. His hands were silent on the lock. And then they were out the door.

"I want you to run as fast as you can to the next farmhouse. Whatever happens, don't stop running. When you get there, call the sheriff's office. If anything happens to me, you keep running. You got that?"

Leigh nodded. But in her heart she knew that if anything happened to Jake she wouldn't leave him. She glanced through the lightly falling snow at the faint lights in the distance. The neighboring farm had to be at least two miles away.

"Let's go," he said, and pulled her into a dead run.

Chapter Seven

Jake ran hard. He knew he was pushing Leigh to the limit of her physical capabilities. But he also knew what would happen if Rasmussen captured them. He'd seen the man's handiwork, and he swore that was the one thing he would not let happen.

It seemed to take forever to reach the neighboring farm. They plowed through high grass and dry corn and snow. The frigid air burned his lungs as if someone had poured acid down his throat. He could feel Leigh lagging, so he took her hand and dragged her, praying she didn't fall.

"What are we going to do without a vehicle?" she panted. "We can't run like this much farther."

"Let's just hope we find one we can borrow."

They approached the farm from the rear, running between the barn and grain silo. An old Chevy truck sat in the driveway. Not his first choice for a getaway vehicle, but then, he was in no position to be choosy. He darted to the truck. Relief poured through him when the door opened. He checked the visor for keys, found none and swore.

Nearby, a dog began to bark.

Jake used the butt of his gun to shatter the steering column. Kneeling, he found the ignition wires and touched them together. The engine groaned. "This damn cold isn't helping."

"The lights just came on in the house," Leigh said.

No time to look. He tried the wires again. The truck coughed like a sick cow. He was aware of the dog howling frantically now. Of Leigh speaking to him. Of the fear in her voice. Of that same fear stealing through his own body. Not for himself, but for her. If Rasmussen got a hold of them, neither would survive, and death would be very slow in coming.

Finally the engine turned over. White exhaust spewed into the air. "Get in."

He shoved her onto the seat, then climbed behind the wheel. Jamming the truck into gear he hit the gas. The vehicle fishtailed. Lights flashed on. In his peripheral vision Jake saw an old man with a shotgun dashing out of the house.

"Damn!"

A shotgun blast punctuated his words. The rear window shattered. Leigh yelped. "Get down!" Jake shouted and shoved her to the seat.

He left the driveway. The truck bounced wildly through the plowed field. Too fast, but Jake knew if he slowed they would get stuck in the snow. In the distance he saw headlights at the vacant house where they'd been ambushed. Several vehicles.

The truck lurched into a drainage ditch. The floorboards scraped against the frozen earth. When the vehicle vaulted onto a road, Jake cut the wheel, using the telephone poles on either side of the road to guide him.

"Why aren't they coming after us?"

He glanced over at Leigh. She was turned

in the seat, her eyes glued to the road behind them. Even in the dim light coming off the dash he could see that she was shivering. Whether it was from cold or fear or both, he couldn't say. Frigid air poured in through the broken window. Reaching down, he turned on the heater.

"I don't know." Then he silently prayed Rasmussen's men wouldn't hurt that old farmer. He looked in the rearview mirror. "We were lucky to get out of there."

"The farmer saw us. He'll call the police, won't he?"

"If Rasmussen's thugs don't kill him."

She put her hand to her mouth. "Oh, no."

"If the old man does get to the phone, the police are going to be looking for this truck." He didn't mention that no matter how well trained local law enforcement were, they wouldn't stand a chance against Rasmussen's men, who were armed with automatic weapons and a complete lack of conscience.

"Jake, how did they know where to find us?"

The question had been nagging at him like a bad toothache. How indeed? Should he voice his concerns? But he knew this was no time for secrecy. If something happened to him, she would be on her own. She would need every resource in order to survive.

"That's the ten-thousand-dollar question," he said.

Her eyes searched his. "They couldn't possibly have followed us. How could they have known we were in that farmhouse?"

"Only two ways I can think of," he said. "Rasmussen could have traced the call."

"Isn't that sophisticated for him?"

"Not for Rasmussen. He's connected. This area is desolate. Using triangulation, he could have narrowed down the cell tower."

She seemed to consider that a moment. "What's the other way?"

He didn't want to think what he was thinking. But the thought was in his head, growing like a cancer. "There was only one person I spoke with."

"My God. You spoke with one of the agents from MIDNIGHT."

"Yeah." Bitterness laced the word. He'd trusted Mike Madrid with his life. With Leigh's life. Was it possible Ian Rasmussen had gotten to him? Threatened him in some way to gain his cooperation? Or had Madrid betrayed him and his oath to the agency for the likes of money?

"Why would someone with the agency betray you?"

"Maybe Rasmussen got to him, threatened him in some way. Threatened his family." But even as he said the words, they didn't sit well. Madrid wasn't the kind of man to be used in that way. Unless he was protecting someone. But Madrid didn't have a wife or children. Who would he be protecting?

"Rasmussen could have offered him money."

Jake didn't want to believe that, but knew it was something he had to consider. "We're on our own," he said.

He didn't miss the shiver that ran through her body, and he wanted to put his arms around her, draw her against him and keep her safe. At least until Rasmussen was captured. But deep inside, Jake knew that wouldn't be enough. Leigh was under his skin. Time hadn't dulled his feelings or his attraction to her. No matter how things turned out, he knew he would never get her out of his system.

He recalled the kiss they'd shared back at the farmhouse, and his body stirred with an uncomfortable intensity. Shifting in the seat, he wondered if she had been affected as profoundly as he had. Probably not, he thought, and reminded himself she was off-limits for too many reasons to count, let alone that she blamed him for using her to get to Rasmussen.

But not even knowing all that could keep the sweet promise of her body from torturing him.

"How did they get away?"

The words were spoken calmly, but Ian Rasmussen was as far from calm as a man could get.

"The plan was to strike when they were asleep and ambush them." Derrick LeValley lifted a shoulder, let it fall. "They slipped out the back and somehow made it to a neighboring farm."

"They fled on foot?"

"They stole a vehicle."

"You should have had them surrounded."

"We stormed the house. The plan was to overwhelm them quick—"

"I've grown tired of your excuses." Rasmussen shook his head in disbelief. "I do not tolerate failure."

"We'll get them, Mr. Rasmussen. Vanderpol might be good, but he can't elude us much longer."

"The longer I stay on this continent, the greater the chance of my being apprehended by the police." Rasmussen ground his teeth. "I will not go back to prison. And I will not leave without taking care of them."

"I can assure you, we'll—"

Rasmussen sliced his hand through the air, silencing the other man. He was tired of talk, of promises not being delivered. More to the point, he was tired of being on the run. Much like the prison he'd just escaped from, it was interfering with the lifestyle he was accustomed to. He'd planned on being at his secret villa on the Moroccan coast by now. Because of Leigh Michaels and Jake Vanderpol, that had not happened.

"Do you have even the slightest idea where they are?" he asked.

"We know they're in Missouri. Maybe Illinois."

Turning away from his employee, he strode to the window and looked out at the snow-covered street below. He'd made it across the Canadian border during the night. It had cost him twenty thousand dollars, but the border patrol had let them pass. Ian had wanted to kill the son of a bitch for charging so much. But he didn't want to draw attention to himself. There would be time for revenge later.

He went over to the table and poured tea into a Wedgwood cup. The King Edward hotel was one of the best in Toronto, but he didn't notice the fine china or elegant furnishings. All he cared about was getting his hands on Leigh Michaels and that bastard Vanderpol. He could not leave this unfinished. He could not leave knowing they were together. Knowing she had betrayed him not once, but twice. That she was giving her body to another man. That they were laughing at him behind his back....

The thought filled him with such rage that his vision blurred. He flung the cup and saucer across the room. "I want them caught! I want it done yesterday. The next man who screws up dies." He turned to LeValley. "Are we clear?"

LeValley shifted nervously. "Crystal."

A tense minute ticked by. LeValley cleared his throat and motioned toward the cell phone he'd purchased just that morning. "Our contact at the phone company is standing by."

"I'll make the call." Rasmussen turned to his employee. "Don't rely on the trace to find them. I want you to dig up everything you can on both of them. Find out who their friends are. Where their families live. Where they might go. Do whatever it takes. Spare no resources. I want them found."

"They won't elude us again."

"I'll believe that when I have Jake Vander- pol's blood on my hands."

LEIGH DIDN'T KNOW how she managed to fall asleep. It was too damn cold to do much of anything except shiver. But somehow she dozed. She was dreaming about Jake when the chirp of her cell phone jerked her awake. Star- tled, she sat up and looked around. It was dawn, and they were stopped at a gas station in the middle of nowhere, surrounded by dry corn and brittle winter trees. Jake was pumping gas.

She unclipped the phone from her belt. Confusion swelled when she noticed the name of one of her co-workers on the display. "Hello?"

"If you want to live you'll listen to what I have to say."

A chill that had nothing to do with the temperature shuddered through her at the sound of Rasmussen's voice. "You tried to kill us last night," she said. "Why would I listen to anything you have to say?"

"It's you I want, Leigh, not Vanderpol."

She was trembling so hard she could barely hear him. In the back of her mind, she remembered Jake telling her not to speak to Rasmussen on the phone. But how had he gotten a hold of her co-worker's phone?

"If you want to save his life, come to me. You know I won't hurt you. It's the only way I'll let him live."

"I don't believe you."

"If I find you with him, you will hear every single one of his screams as he dies a slow and painful death. Is that what you want?"

"I want you to leave us alone."

"You and I have unfinished business. I have no quarrel with Vanderpol. If you want him to live you'll meet with me."

She felt the phone shaking against her ear. She heard her heart thundering in her ears.

"Have you slept with him?" he whispered.

Leigh disconnected and sagged against the seat.

"Who the hell were you talking to?"

Somehow she found her voice. "Rasmussen just called."

"Damn it, I told you not to talk to him."

"The display said the call was from one of my co-workers back in Denver," she said. "How did he manage that?"

The dark look Jake gave her said it all.

Leigh felt sick. "Please tell me he didn't hurt them."

"We don't know that," Jake said. "Rasmussen could have had one of his thugs steal the phone." He reached for her phone. "How long did you talk?"

"Less than a minute."

"He could have traced the call." His eyes narrowed. "What did he say?"

"N-nothing."

"Nothing seems to have you pretty shaken up." He paused. "What did he say?"

"He says if I meet with him, he'll let you live."

Jake dropped her cell phone onto the pavement and crushed it beneath his boot.

Leigh couldn't get Rasmussen's voice out of her head. *If I find you with him, you will hear every single one of his screams as he dies a slow and painful death.*

"Leigh."

He touched her arm. She glanced at him. He'd slid onto the seat beside her and was looking at her with sympathy in his eyes. "He'll say anything to get what he wants. Don't believe any of it."

"He wants me, Jake. Not you."

"He wants both of us."

"He said…" Her voice cracked. "He said if I don't go to him he'll kill you."

Jake ran his hand up and down her arm. "He's not going to kill either of us. Rasmussen is an international criminal. He can't hide out indefinitely. He's going to screw up, and someone's going to bring him down."

"He's incredibly connected and wealthy. He uses both of those things to buy his way."

"Not everyone can be bought."

Like you, she thought with a small tinge of pride.

He slid his hand from her arm. "We've got to keep moving."

"Where are we going?"

"The only safe place I can think of."

JAKE MADE THE CALL he'd been dreading, while Leigh freshened up and bought coffee. He dialed Sean Cutter's personal number. A number he knew was secure.

"It's Vanderpol."

A beat of silence. "Where's my witness?"

"With me. Safe."

"That's not what I hear from the Kansas State Police."

Damn. Cutter knew about the ambush at the farmhouse. "Mike Madrid is the only person who knew where we were."

Another beat of silence. "What are you saying?"

"I'm saying draw your own conclusions."

"You think Madrid gave you up?"

Jake sighed. "I don't want to think that, but how the hell else did Rasmussen find us? That house was out in the middle of nowhere."

"He's got a lot of resources, Jake."

"Yeah, well, so do I." Jake sighed unhappily. "Rasmussen has made contact with her twice."

"Conceivably, he could have traced the call."

"He'd have to know someone at the phone company."

"I'll see what I can find out. If he makes contact again—"

"I destroyed the phone."

"We could have used it."

"Not at the risk of his finding her."

Cutter sighed. "Jake, bring her in. Let us take her until this bastard is caught."

It was the logical thing to do. But Jake had never been all that logical when it came to Leigh. He knew what would happen when he took her in. They would take her to an undisclosed location. He would be excluded because as of the day before he was no longer an agent. Her safety would be out of his control....

"Someone hacked the system, Cutter. She's going to be safer with me."

"Rasmussen smells blood, damn it."

"I'll handle this."

"The way you did the last time?" Cutter asked.

The punch of guilt was quick and brutal. "I delivered Rasmussen to you." *At what cost?* a nagging little voice asked.

"Come on, Jake. Bring her in. Let us handle this."

Jake disconnected without responding.

Chapter Eight

Jake stuck to the back roads, and by late afternoon they'd crossed the Illinois state line. Leigh had no idea where he was taking her. At this point she thought it didn't matter. As long as Rasmussen couldn't find them.

But she knew they were only buying time. Rasmussen wouldn't stop looking for her.

If I find you with him, you will hear every single one of his screams as he dies a slow and painful death.

She couldn't get those words out of her head. In the years since she'd been with Rasmussen, she'd researched him. The things she'd learned about the man she'd once thought she loved sickened her. Beneath the charismatic charm lay a monster with a black heart and a thirst for blood. He dealt in death.

Weapons sold to the highest bidder no matter what their intent.

"We need to talk about what happened six years ago."

It was the last thing she'd expected Jake to say. It was the last thing she wanted to talk about. Not when she was both physically and mentally exhausted. "I've put it behind me, Jake. Maybe you should, too."

"I want you to understand why I did what I did."

"I understand all too well what happened."

"If you did you wouldn't look at me like that."

"Like what?"

"Like you expect a knife in the back at any moment."

"Isn't that what you *did?* Put a knife in my back?"

His hands flexed on the wheel. "Not by a long shot."

"You manipulated me."

"I didn't manipulate you. I sure as hell didn't use you."

"You slept with me. You made me believe

you cared. Then later I find out that all along you'd been planning to wire me for sound and send me back to Ian. What would you call it?"

"I came up with that plan before—" He bit off the sentence, his jaw clamping shut. "Before I...before we became involved."

"And that makes it all right?" She lowered her voice in a poor imitation of his. "Oh, if I've slept with her, I can't send her into the lion's den. But if I haven't slept with her, then it's okay to risk a woman's life as long as I get my man."

"How many times do I have to tell you? I did try to abort the sting," he said. "But you had your own ideas, didn't you?"

"I knew I was the best way to get to him. But I hated you for thinking of using me that way. Especially after—" *Everything we shared,* a cruel little voice chimed in. But Leigh couldn't say the words. She didn't want Jake to know just how profoundly he'd touched her in the few short days they'd spent together. She would never open herself up like that again.

"I didn't know you when I came up with the plan. I thought you were—" He glanced over at her. "I thought you were like him. I thought you were part of his organization. I thought you could handle it. Besides, there were agents standing by. If you'd gotten into trouble they could have been there in two minutes."

"A lot can happen in two minutes."

His gaze meeting hers flashed a dark emotion she couldn't quite read. "You were with him a hell of a lot longer than two minutes."

Leigh felt herself flush and looked away. She'd never told Jake what had happened the night Sean Cutter had wired her for sound and sent her into Ian Rasmussen's North Michigan Avenue penthouse. She'd never told another living soul. But she knew several of the agents at MIDNIGHT Agency knew. After all, they'd been listening in while she'd sold her soul. While she'd gotten Rasmussen to incriminate himself. But it had cost her something precious. A piece of herself she would never be able to recoup....

"Don't you dare condemn me for what I did." Her voice shook with anger. Shame and self-recrimination rose inside her. It had taken her six years to realize the wounds Ian

Rasmussen had put on her soul would never fully heal. The best she could hope for, she'd realized, was that someday she would learn to live with them.

JAKE WASN'T SURE which was worse, knowing that she'd slept with Rasmussen to induce an incriminating statement, or knowing he was partly responsible.

He'd never been a jealous man. But the thought of Leigh with Rasmussen made him see red. Made him feel like a son of a bitch because the sting had been *his* idea. After all, Jake Vanderpol always got his man. No matter what the price. No matter who got hurt. In this case, he figured everyone involved had seen plenty of hurt, especially Leigh.

"I'm sorry," he said after a moment.

A breath shuddered out of her. When she turned to him, her eyes were so haunted it hurt him to look into them. "It's done," she said. "Over. In the past. I did what I did. But so did you, Jake."

Judging from the pain etched into her features, he figured the ordeal wouldn't be over for her for a long time to come. "You did an incredibly brave thing, Leigh. I'm sorry you had to do it, but your going back to Rasmussen was courageous."

"I don't know what I was thinking, getting involved with him in the first place." She shook her head. "I was incredibly stupid."

"You were twenty-one years old. You'd been in Chicago for what? A month? You didn't have a lot of life experience to draw upon." He ought to know. He'd been the one to develop her profile when he'd originally planned the sting. She'd been ideal.

Remembering, Jake sighed. Six years ago, fresh off the family farm in Iowa, she'd been attending college and working part-time at Rasmussen's North Michigan Avenue restaurant. Within the first week, Rasmussen had begun wooing her. Buying her expensive gifts. Sending her flowers. Showing her extravagant nights on the town. Back then, Leigh had had no reason to be suspicious of the charismatic restaurateur. Two months later she was living in his lavish penthouse. Her idyllic world had come crashing down when she'd discovered her boyfriend was an international arms dealer. She'd called the police, who had then passed her on to the FBI. Eventually, the MIDNIGHT Agency had been called in. Jake had been assigned the case. He hadn't anticipated falling for the woman he'd been assigned to protect....

Pulling his mind from thoughts that never ceased to torment him, he turned his attention back to his driving. At some point it had begun to snow. Just flurries, but Jake knew the Great Lakes to the north could bring on blizzardlike conditions with little or no warning.

He glanced over at Leigh and, as always, was taken aback by her beauty. He understood all too well why a man like Rasmussen could become obsessed with her. She was lovely and kind with a strong spirit. Six years ago, after only a few days, Jake had been in miles over his head. It was the one and only case he'd ever become personally involved in. The one and only witness with whom he'd crossed a line. The operation had nearly cost him his job. It had definitely cost him his peace of mind.

"We'll stop at the next town for food and gas."

The words were barely out of his mouth

when he caught a glimpse in the rearview mirror of a white SUV—no headlights, dark windshield bearing down on them at a dangerous speed.

"Hold on!" he shouted.

An instant later the SUV slammed into the truck's bumper. The pickup skidded sideways. Jake fought the wheel, muscling the vehicle back onto the road.

"Where did he come from?" Leigh cried, glancing through the rear window.

"Visibility is low because of the snow." Jake barely had time to brace before the SUV's bumper crashed into the pickup a second time. He steered into the skid and regained control. A light veneer of snow coated the road, making the asphalt slick. He checked his speed, but before he could take his foot off the gas, the SUV slammed into them a third time. The momentum sent the truck into a wild spin.

Leigh screamed as the truck careened into the drainage ditch.

Jake looked over at Leigh. "Are you all right?"

Her face was nearly as white as the snow, but she nodded. "I'm fine."

He glanced out his window to see the SUV turning around a hundred yards away. *He's coming back to finish us off,* he thought, and swore he would not let Rasmussen get his hands on Leigh.

The engine had died. Jake slid down and hot-wired the ignition. The engine coughed and then turned over. Ramming the gearshift into Reverse, he floored the gas, tried to get the truck rocking, but his efforts were in vain.

Jake punched the dash. "We're stuck."

Leigh looked through the rear window. "They're coming back."

He unsheathed his pistol. "Take this."

Leigh's eyes widened as he slid the weapon into her hand. "Jake, my God…"

"I want you to empty the clip into the front window, driver's side. You've got eleven shots. Don't count them. Pull the trigger until you're out." Taking her right hand in his, he leveled the weapon at the SUV that was now speeding toward them. "It's our only chance."

She jerked her head once.

Ripping off his safety belt, Jake threw open his door and stumbled from the truck. "Open fire!" he shouted. "Now!"

Shots erupted as he tore his jacket from his body, set it beneath the rear tire of the truck and then scrambled behind the wheel.

"There's a second SUV!" Terror laced her voice.

Jake glanced out the rearview mirror to see the first SUV nosedown into the drainage ditch. Fifty yards in the opposite direction, a second SUV sped toward them.

"Damn it!" Praying his jacket did the trick, he jammed the truck into Reverse and hit the gas. The wheels spun for an instant, then caught. The truck zoomed backward.

But the second SUV was already upon them. He heard gunshots. At first he thought Leigh had some ammunition left and was putting it to good use. Then a bullet blew a hole the size of his fist through the left-front fender.

"Get down!"

Not waiting for Leigh to comply, he used his right hand to push her to the floor. He reached for his pistol on the seat, brought it up. The first shot missed its mark. The second shot shattered the windshield. The third shot exploded the front right tire.

Dropping the weapon onto the seat, Jake twisted the steering wheel and floored the accelerator.

When he looked over at Leigh, he saw blood and his heart virtually stopped.

Chapter Nine

"Leigh!"

Jake had been in a lot of tight situations in the years he'd been with the MIDNIGHT Agency. But nothing he'd experienced compared with the gut punch of terror that went through him at the sight of blood coming through her coat.

She was kneeling on the floor, grimacing as she climbed onto the seat. One look at her face and his stomach dropped into his shoes. She was pale. Too pale. And all he could think was that she was seriously injured and bleeding out right before his eyes.

"My God, are you all right?"

Not waiting for an answer, he leaned over and set his hand on her back. Panicked, he couldn't stop staring at the amount of blood on her jacket, on his hand, a bright-red stain that was spreading. Oh, dear God, it had to be bad.

"Oh, honey." Jake glanced back at the road just in time to keep the truck from veering into a ditch.

"Jake, I don't think it's bad."

He didn't believe it. Bullet wounds could be deceiving, especially once shock set in. Getting her hurt was the one thing he'd sworn he wouldn't let happen.

Screwed it up again, didn't you, hotshot?

The need to stop the truck and check her out, make sure she wasn't badly hurt, tugged at him. But he knew the situation would become even more deadly if Rasmussen's men captured them. A flat tire was only going to buy a small window of time. He intended to make the best of it.

"Where are you hit?" he asked.

"The back of my shoulder."

He glanced at her. His stomach went queasy at the sight of the blood. *Her* blood. "How do you feel? Are you dizzy? Hot?"

"Scared spitless."

"You're going to be all right. I promise."

He gripped the wheel hard. "Are you hurting?"

"Starting to, but it'll wait."

He didn't think so. "I'm going to find a place to pull over."

"If you pull over, they'll catch us."

Taking in the falling snow, he almost smiled. "No, they won't."

It was nearly an hour before he found a suitable place to stop. Suitable being a relevant term. It was a deserted grain elevator outside Decatur, Illinois. Jake chose it because there was a covered pass-through where trucks were loaded with grain and weighed. It was out of sight from the road. Shelter from the storm. With a little luck, they might just survive the night.

He pulled the truck into the lot and drove to the pass-through and shut down the engine. Next to him, Leigh sat quietly. She'd remained calm and upbeat in the hour it had taken him to find the elevator. He knew she was trying not to worry him. But Jake saw the pain and worry etched into her features. And it tore him up inside because this was his fault.

Maybe he should have turned her over to MIDNIGHT instead of trying to handle it on his own. But he doubted even they could keep her safe. Rasmussen had hacked into the Witness Security Program database. Something Jake and everyone else had always considered impossible. If Mike Madrid had given up Jake's location, could Jake really trust anyone within the agency?

The question nagged at him as he slid from the truck and opened the passenger door for Leigh. One look at her face and he knew she was hurting. That she was scared. He prayed the pale cast of her complexion wasn't a sign of serious bleeding or shock.

"Come on, honey." Before even realizing he was going to reach for her, she was in his arms.

"You don't have to carry me," she said.

"Better if you don't move around too much until I assess that wound."

Though it wasn't yet five o'clock, it was nearly dark. Snow fell heavily from a brooding sky. The wind had picked up, and he could hear it howling throughout the old grain elevator. They needed shelter from the cold and wind and snow. He spotted the door to what had once been the office and headed toward it.

To his surprise the old door was unlocked. He pushed it open with a booted foot. A dusty counter stood to his left. Straight ahead, wood shelves warped with age lined the wall. A window with a crack straight down the center looked out over the drive-through where the trucks had once been loaded and weighed.

"Have the bellman bring our things around."

He looked down at her, wondering if she were falling into delirium.

"That was a joke," she said.

Jake didn't laugh. "Can you stand?"

"Of course I can."

Some of the color had returned to her face. Up until this moment he'd been too concerned about her physical condition to think about just how good she felt in his arms. But looking into the crystal blue of her eyes, the rightness of it struck him hard.

She was small and soft against him, and his body responded the way it always did when she was close. Six years ago he hadn't been able to resist her. Holed up in a safe house for days on end, their mutual attraction had quickly spiraled out of control—and into something magical. He knew she hadn't forgiven him. But right or wrong, the sharp-edged attraction was still there. So was the magic.

Knowing better than to get caught up in a situation that would only end up hurting them both, he carried Leigh to the counter and let her slide to her feet. He watched her closely for a wobble, but she stood straight with her shoulders back, her chin high.

"If you're waiting for me to collapse, it's not going to happen," she said.

"In that case, I'll let you stand here while I go get the first-aid kit."

"Jake, I'm going to be okay."

Because the bullet wound was on the backside of her shoulder, he figured she hadn't yet seen the amount of blood. "If you have a bullet in you, we're going to the hospital."

"We could just send Rasmussen an invitation to come kill us."

"You don't mess around with bullet wounds, Leigh. You know that."

She turned away from him but not before

he noticed that she'd once again gone pale. "Take off your jacket," he said. "Drape it over your shoulders to conserve body heat. I'll be right back with the kit."

The snow was blowing sideways when Jake walked to the truck to retrieve the kit. The bad weather was a mixed blessing. While it would conceal their tire tracks and slow down Rasmussen's men, it would also hinder his own travel if he needed to get Leigh to the hospital or leave quickly.

Jake returned with the first-aid kit, an extra blanket, the last two bottles of water and a flashlight. Leigh had just finished clearing off the counter and turned toward him when he entered.

Looking at her, it occurred to him that she was going to have to remove her shirt for him to take a look at that wound. Now that the tables were turned, and she was the injured one, he was just as uncomfortable with Leigh's getting undressed in front of him as he'd been earlier when he'd had to do the same. He vowed not to let the sight of her pretty body get to him.

Still, he flushed as he set the kit on the

counter. "Why don't you hop up on the counter. I'll rig the flashlight and take a look."

She looked as if she wanted to argue. But while Leigh might be stubborn and argumentative at times, she wasn't stupid. "All right."

Not waiting for her to move, Jake put his hands beneath her arms. She seemed weightless as he lifted her onto the counter. Despite his vow not to let her get to him, the sweet scent of her hair titillated his senses, and his heart beat faster. Their eyes met briefly, long enough for him to feel the quick rise of heat between them.

He propped the flashlight against the shelf, rigging it so that the beam shone in the general direction of her shoulder. Once the light was in place, he turned to her. "You're going to have to take off your shirt."

She looked at him as if he'd asked her to stick her neck in a guillotine. Then her gaze skittered away and she looked everywhere except for into his eyes.

"I'll turn around," he said. "You can drape the blanket over your shoulders."

"Okay."

He turned away. Clothing rustled as she

removed her shirt. He closed his eyes against the quick swipe of desire. In his mind's eye he saw her the way he'd seen her six years ago. She'd been innocence and passion and heat like he'd never before known. She'd shared every inch of her body with him. There had been no hesitation, no vacillation. It was as if they'd known their time was limited.

The regrets had come later, he thought.

"Okay."

Bracing himself, Jake turned slowly toward her. But nothing could prepare him for her beauty. She was sitting on the counter, facing him. The blanket was draped over her shoulders, the ends clutched together just above her breasts so hard her knuckles were white. His eyes were drawn to the slender angle of her throat. His imagination filled in the rest.

He went instantly hard. His vow went straight out the window. The rush of blood to his groin was so powerful that he felt dizzy and hot and for an instant he wondered if he was coming down with something. Then he remembered it had always

been like this between them. Well, back
when she hadn't hated him, anyway.

Jake cleared his throat and shifted his
weight from one foot to the other to accom-
modate his erection. "Swivel around and let
me have a look at the back part of your shoulder."

She winced when she turned, and Jake
reached out to help her slide around. Once her
back was to him, he took the edge of the blanket and gently lowered it.

She had a beautiful back. All golden skin
and silky, slender shoulders. Then the bullet
wound came into view and he went queasy.

"Aw, Leigh." On impulse, he reached out
and set his hand against her shoulder and
turned her slightly so that the light illumi-
nated the wound.

"Bad?" she asked.

"I'll know as soon as I get it cleaned up."
Using his finger, he gently slid her bra strap
from her shoulder. "This is going to sting."

"I can take it."

He moistened a gauze pad with hydrogen
peroxide and wiped away the blood that

stained the skin surrounding the wound. "Bled a lot," he said.

Her quick intake of breath told him it hurt when he touched the wound. "Sorry. Gotta do this."

"Sadist."

He moistened a fresh gauze pad. Relief trickled through him when he realized the bullet had just grazed her. "It's just a nick." *Thank God.*

"If a graze hurts this much, I'd hate to find out what it feels like to get shot."

"I'm not going to let that happen."

She looked at him over her shoulder, and Jake resisted the urge to pull her to him and make promises he knew he might not be able to keep. "You could probably use a couple of stitches."

"Sorry, Vanderpol, but I draw the line at your jabbing a needle into me. My turn, I guess, for a butterfly bandage. Can you make it quick? It's getting a little drafty."

Looking at the smooth flesh of the most perfect female back he'd ever seen, Jake couldn't have disagreed more. As far as he was concerned, it was getting downright hot.

The thought sent another rush of blood to his groin and he nearly groaned with frustration. Shifting, he reached for a small tube of antibiotic cream. "You've got some bruising," he said in a rough voice. "You're going to be hurting for a few days."

"Both of us are going to be hurting if Rasmussen gets that close again," she said.

"I don't plan on letting that happen."

"You didn't plan on letting that happen the first time."

She winced when Jake affixed the bandage. "Sorry."

"Jake, we can't keep running like this. We have to come up with a plan."

He debated whether to tell her about his suspicions with regard to Mike Madrid and the MIDNIGHT Agency. He didn't want to frighten her unduly. But Jake was a realist; she had good reason to be frightened. She deserved the truth. If something happened to him it might save her life.

"I'm fresh out of plans, Leigh."

"We're going to run out of places to hide. These bullets are getting a little too close for comfort. First you, now me."

"Right now running is the only thing that's keeping us alive. We can't rely on the Witness Security Program. Not until we find out what happened."

"Jake, I don't understand why you haven't contacted your people at the MID-NIGHT Agency."

"I told you. I left the agency. They wanted me to put you in the hands of another agency and I told them to get screwed." Not that he'd done a stellar job of protecting her so far.

"I understand. But that doesn't mean the men and women you work with aren't good. I'm not exactly comfortable putting my fate in the hands of someone else but, Jake, what other choices are there?"

"I still think someone within the agency gave up our location," he said.

She turned to him, her eyes wide with shock. "Who would do such a thing?"

"I don't know. Maybe they were threatened. Maybe they did it for money." Jake ground his teeth at the thought.

She bit her lip. "Who? Do you know?"

"I'm not sure about any of this—"

"Judging from the look on your face you have a pretty good idea."

Jake looked away. "Mike Madrid."

She blinked. "He's your friend."

"That's what makes this so damn difficult."

"Jake, twenty-four hours ago I thought I could handle this on my own. I thought I could disappear. A new town. A new identity. A new life. But after everything that's happened, I'm not so sure."

"I knew from the start we were in over our heads. Do you have any idea how difficult it would have been to hack into the Witness Security Program?"

"If anyone could pull it off, Rasmussen can. He's a multimillionaire, Jake. He has resources and power. If someone refuses to cooperate, he either buys them or kills them."

"Or their family." Frustrated and more scared than he wanted to admit—not for himself, but for Leigh—he said, "If he got to Mike Madrid, he can get to anybody. I know Mike. He's not for sale. For him to give us up, it would have to be bad."

"Does he have family?"

"He never talks about his family or his past."

"What makes you think he sold you out?"

"He was the only person who knew where we were last night."

She considered that a moment. "Ian called me, Jake. Maybe he traced the call."

"It's possible, but he'd practically have to own the phone company to do that."

"Maybe he does."

"Still, I don't think we should rely on MIDNIGHT to bail us out of this."

"That's why we need to come up with a plan."

So they were back to the plan. Jake had to admire her strength. She'd been threatened and shot at and on the run for days. And yet she wasn't falling to pieces. "What do you have in mind?"

"We know what he wants. Let's dangle it in front of him and see if he bites."

Jake felt a sinking sensation in his gut. "Don't even go there, Leigh."

"Use me as bait."

"No." The single word was out of his

mouth before he could stop it. A decision made on emotion, something he'd only done once before in his life. It was ironic as hell the only other time he'd acted on emotion alone, it had been with regard to this woman.

"It worked six years ago, why wouldn't it work now?" she asked.

"Things were different six years ago."

"You still want Ian Rasmussen. He still wants me. I don't see that things have changed that much."

Except I can't bear the thought of your getting hurt. He banked the thought before he could voice it. "He wants to hurt you, Leigh."

"He hurt me six years ago and that didn't stop you."

Jake wasn't proud of the way things had gone down six years ago. He felt sick with guilt every time he thought of what he'd put her through. He swore he wouldn't make the same mistake twice.

"I'm sorry you got hurt."

"Sorry isn't going to keep us alive."

Needing to look into her eyes, to make her understand, he grasped her shoulders and gently turned her to face him. He'd almost forgotten that she'd removed her shirt. But she was clutching the blanket to her breast as if it were a lifeline.

"Six years ago it was all about the job," he said. "It was about me getting my suspect. Good against evil. Black and white. You were with him. I thought you were like him." Looking into her eyes, he couldn't imagine how he'd ever believed that about her. "Then, when I was assigned to protect you, when we were together in that safe house for five days—" he looked away, then forced his gaze back to hers "—when I got to know you, everything changed."

Her eyes searched his. Tears shimmered in their depths, but she didn't let them spill. If only she would open up to him, believe him. Forgive him.

"You slept with me," she said. "Then you sent me back to Rasmussen. You knew what I'd have to do, but you didn't care."

"That's not true," Jake shot back. "I didn't mean for things to get complicated between us."

She blinked back tears. "I had to sleep

with him." A sob escaped her. "It's the worst thing I've ever had to do in my life."

Jake felt the words like a punch to the solar plexus. He'd spent six unbearable years wondering what had gone down that night.

The harsh reality of what she'd had to do—of what he was partially responsible for—hurt far more than he ever could have imagined.

Chapter Ten

Leigh had never forgiven Jake. She'd given him her body, her heart. She'd fallen in love with him. In turn he'd hurt her so deeply that she'd thought she'd never recover.

But he wasn't the only one at fault. She'd found out about the plan from another agent, who'd told her the sting had been Jake's idea. She hadn't given Jake the chance to change his mind. She'd told herself then she'd gone along with the plan because she'd known it was the only way to stop Rasmussen. But as time passed, she'd finally admitted to herself that a part of her had also wanted to hurt Jake because he'd been the one to devise the plan. So was it really fair to continue to hold that against him?

"By the time I found out Cutter was going

to go through with the plan, you were already wired and on your way to Rasmussen's penthouse," Jake said.

He grasped her arms and forced her gaze to his. "I tried to stop it, Leigh, but Cutter wouldn't pull you in." He sighed. "We came to blows over it. Two agents had to pull me off. I came within an inch of losing my job with the agency."

"Jake, I'd never felt so...used. So alone in my entire life."

He could only imagine how terrifying it must have been for her being alone with a killer. The wire the agency had used was the size of a safety pin and hidden in an earring. But if Rasmussen had found out what she was doing, he would have killed her before an agent could have gotten in to save her.

"You were in that penthouse for five hours." He'd been wild with fear for her safety for every second of those torturously long five hours.

"It seemed like forever," she said.

He ran his hands up and down her arms. "Cutter had put me on administrative leave. I didn't know where you were. I couldn't listen in, and I was insane with worry." His gaze went to hers. "And sick with guilt."

Even now the thought of her being with the international arms dealer filled him with a rage so black he could barely contain it. "I'm sorry you had to go through that," he said. "I'm sorry I hurt you. But I can tell you, Leigh, it nearly killed me knowing you were with him. That you'd risked your life."

That they were facing the same thing now filled him with dread.

"I'm not going to let you do it again," he whispered.

"It's not your decision to make."

"It's my decision as long as I'm breathing."

"You know it's the only way to stop him."

"It's too dangerous. I'm not going to let you risk your life."

"I'm not going to let him destroy what's left of my life." She turned away and slid from the counter. She'd only taken two steps when Jake stopped her.

"Don't walk away from me," he growled, snagging her uninjured arm.

"Don't try to run my life or tell me what

to do. I know this isn't going to be easy. I know it's dangerous. But what's the alternative?"

When he pulled her to him, he was suddenly aware of heat and curves and the softness of her body against his. Temptation speared him. Looking into her eyes, he found the last six years had melted away. Six years of missing her and wondering where she was. Wondering if she ever thought of him and the magic they had shared.

Jake didn't intend to kiss her. Getting this close to her when his emotions were running high, his body was running hot, was like tossing a match into a keg of gunpowder. But even knowing what was at stake—her safety, her very life—he could no more resist her now than he could six years ago.

Knowing his fate was sealed, he lowered his mouth to hers.

JAKE'S MOUTH ON HERS was like the arc of a thousand volts of electricity between two conductors. Every nerve ending in her body sizzled with pleasure.

Leigh knew better than to let herself be

swept away. But Jake Vanderpol was one weakness she'd never been able to resist.

As his mouth seared hers, her only thought was that she'd been wrong about him. About what he'd done. A door that had been slammed shut and locked down tight sprang open. Bullet wound forgotten, the past set aside, she wrapped her arms around him. His shoulders were like boulders beneath her hands. She could feel his muscles trembling with restraint. The warmth of his skin chasing away the cold that went all the way to her core.

Growling low in his throat, he raised his hands to her face and kissed her hard. Leigh's mind cried out for her to pull back. To regroup. To take a few minutes to think this through before leaping from a cliff.

But her relationship with Jake had never been rational. It had always been primal and instinctive and out of control. He was the only person in the world who could do that to her, and the intensity of her feelings for him, as they had before, frightened her.

He jammed his fingers through her hair. His tongue entwined with hers. She tasted heat and need, felt the impatient snap of sexual frustration. Pleasure tore down her defenses, rendering her helpless to resist.

Never taking his mouth from hers, he backed her toward the wall, taking, not giving her an inch. A gasp escaped her when her back hit the wall. Her heart **swirled and** dipped when he took her han**ds in his** and lifted them over her head.

"I'm not hurting you, am I?" **he** asked.

"I'm okay."

"Good, because I'm just getting warmed up…"

He kissed her like she'd never been kissed before in her life. Her mouth. Her throat. The tender spot just beneath her ear. Too much intensity. Too many emotions. Too much sensation to absorb.

A protest teetered on her lips. A protest born of the need to protect herself from the hurt he would invariably bring her. That protest came out as a sigh when his body came full length against hers. Leigh whimpered as need took hold of her, as another surge of pleasure overwhelmed her. She was keenly aware of her own body responding to his.

Her heart beat out a maniacal rhythm; her breasts swelled; her nipples hardened and ached to be touched; her panties dampened against her skin.

She could feel the hard ridge of his arousal against her cleft. His labored breaths echoing in her ears. The heat of his mouth against hers. Fire burning her body from the inside out.

She cried out when he brushed his fingertips over her breasts. As if of its own accord, her body arched toward him, wanting him with a desire bordering on madness. She wanted his hands on her breasts, his body inside hers.

It had been six years since she'd been touched by a man. But Leigh didn't want to lose her head the way she had before. She had to stay in control. Six years ago she'd given him the power to hurt her. She couldn't let that happen again.

"Jake," she panted. "Don't."

He stilled, and she used that moment to slip from his grasp. For an instant the only sound came from their labored breathing.

"I'm sorry," she said. "That was a mistake."

"It sure as hell didn't feel like a mistake," he ground out.

"I can't deal with you and...what's happening with Rasmussen at the same time."

"I'm trying to protect you. He's the one trying to hurt you. Don't get the two confused, Leigh."

She hadn't meant it that way, but she didn't correct him. Better to have him angry at her than to have him wanting her. One more kiss and she wasn't sure she would have the strength to stop it.

Cursing beneath his breath, Jake turned away and stalked to the window. Darkness had fallen. He stared out at the snowy landscape, his shoulders broad and square, his spine rigid.

Then he turned to her. As he did, his eyes were cool. "I'm going to pick up some supplies and get gas. I suggest you try to get some rest. We'll leave in three hours."

At that he yanked open the door and stepped into the night.

THE WIND HOWLED around the old grain elevator like a banshee. After an hour of tossing and turning, Jake gave up on sleep. He wasn't sure if it was the physical frustration of wanting Leigh or worry over Rasmussen, but he was too keyed up to rest.

For the life of him he couldn't figure out how Rasmussen was tracking them. Had the international arms dealer traced the calls he'd made to Leigh? Jake didn't see how that was possible, particularly with their being in a rural area.

Or had fellow MIDNIGHT agent Mike Madrid given them up? Jake didn't want to believe that. He'd known Madrid for going on five years. They were friends. Or at least Jake had always thought so. If not a trace— or a mole within the ranks of MIDNIGHT— how was Rasmussen tracking them?

There was only one person he could think of who might be able to help. Fellow MID-NIGHT agent Zack Devlin. Devlin was an undercover operative—and an electronics genius. But with Jake turning in his badge, would the other man help him?

"Only one way to find out," Jake muttered, and unclipped his cell phone.

A glance at the display told him it was

nearly 2:00 a.m. But it didn't matter. MID-NIGHT operatives answered their agency-issue cell phones regardless of the hour.

He dialed Devlin's number from memory. Devlin answered on the fourth ring with an annoyed, "Yeah."

"It's Vanderpol."

The beat of silence that followed told Jake that Devlin knew he'd walked away from the agency. "Any particular reason you're calling me at two o'clock in the freaking morning?"

"I need to know how Rasmussen is tracking us." Jake heard rustling on the other end, the whisper of a feminine voice.

"Kelly sends her best," Devlin said.

"Same goes."

"Jake, why the hell did you walk out? Cutter is frothing-at-the-mouth pissed."

"He was trying to keep me off the case."

"He was bloody right in doing so, man. You're too involved to be thinking clearly."

"They used her to get to Rasmussen last time," Jake snapped. "I wouldn't put it past Cutter to do it again."

"You know as well as I do it's probably the most expeditious way to nab that son of a bitch. Cutter isn't going to let anything happen to her."

I had to sleep with him. Leigh's voice wrenched at him, and Jake closed his eyes.

"Are you going to help me or not?"

"You know I will."

Jake wasn't the only MIDNIGHT agent who'd been known to skate a thin line. "Rasmussen is tracking us. Finding us when I'm certain we haven't been followed."

"Anyone know where you are?"

"Madrid."

An uneasy silence ensued. "I know Mike," Devlin said. "No way."

"Unless they got to his family."

"He doesn't have any family. They were killed."

Jake sighed, not yet convinced. "Rasmussen has called Leigh twice. Maybe he's somehow tracing her cell phone."

"Triangulation will only give the location of the nearest tower, if that."

"We're in a rural area."

"You been shot at?"

The hairs at Jake's nape prickled. "Several times."

Devlin cursed. "There was a new tracking system invented by some Dutch scientists called Micronic GPS. A chip small enough to fit inside a pencil eraser. Two months ago, the firm was broken into. The technology was stolen. Conceivably these chips could be implanted inside a modified projectile."

Now it was Jake's turn to curse. "A projectile the size of a bullet?"

"These modified projectiles are designed to penetrate metal, but not pass through it."

"Jesus."

"Check your vehicle, Jake. Take pliers or wire cutters or a goddamn hammer. Pry open any bullet holes and see if there's a device inside your vehicle. You're looking for a black, plasticlike material that expands on impact. For God's sake, there's a possibility Rasmussen already knows where you are and is waiting for the right time to strike. Go!"

Chapter Eleven

Jake was out of the office and sprinting through the snow toward the old truck even before he hit the end button. He grabbed a big, flathead screwdriver from the truck's bed, twisted it into the nearest bullet hole and pried open the sheet metal. Sure enough a flat, black plastic device clung like melted rubber to the interior mechanics of the driver's-side door.

Praying Devlin had been wrong, he shone the flashlight on the tiny device, surprised to see that his hands were shaking. Even with the naked eye, he could see the copper wiring and solder of the miniature GPS chip.

"Damn it!"

He stood in the lightly falling snow, trying to decide what to do. All the while his eyes scanned the black abyss of the fields and woods surrounding the old grain elevator. He had a bug sweeper that would pick up even the faintest radio frequency, but he'd left it in the Hummer. Should he try to locate and remove the remaining chips? Or should he wake Leigh and make a run for it and hope Rasmussen's thugs weren't within shooting distance?

But it was too cold to get far on foot. He had no choice but to make a sweep of the vehicle and pray he could get every transmitter before they got ambushed.

Starting at the driver's door, Jake swept the flashlight beam over the sheet metal and quickly worked his way toward the rear. He found two additional bullet holes but no transmitters. Not all of the gunmen had been shooting transmitters. He pried open a bullet hole in the tailgate and found a second transmitter and tossed it into the snow. By the time he'd worked his way around the entire truck, he'd located four GPS transmitters.

But if Rasmussen's thugs knew their location, why hadn't they been ambushed?

Jake set his hand against the pistol tucked into his waistband as he jogged back to the building. He went through the front door, then shoved open the office door. He focused the beam where Leigh had been sleeping.

"We need to leave," he said.

His blood turned to ice when he realized she was gone.

LEIGH HAD NEVER LIKED camping for the sole reason that forests didn't come with restroom facilities. Since Jake had been nowhere in sight when she'd wakened a few minutes earlier, she'd made it a point to find a private spot as far away from the grain elevator as safely possible.

Grumbling, she took care of business and was on her way back when the sound of shoes crunching through snow behind her stopped her in her tracks. The thought that it was only Jake walking the perimeter flashed in her mind. But when she spun and saw a man with a gun, she knew venturing out alone had been a very bad idea.

Leigh flung herself into a run. *"Jake!"* She'd taken only a few strides when the man caught her in a flying tackle, his weight knocking her to the ground.

She went down hard. Unable to break her fall, she got a faceful of snow. It was in her eyes. Her nose. Her mouth. She couldn't see, couldn't breathe. Rough arms grasped her wrists from behind. She heard the metallic click of handcuffs and began to panic. Oh, dear God she couldn't let him immobilize her.

She screamed, but the snow muffled the sound. Using every ounce of strength she possessed she twisted, managing to free one arm. Animal sounds tore from her throat as she lashed out at her attacker.

"Hold still, bitch."

Leigh twisted onto her side, kicked out with her right leg. She caught a glimpse of a ski mask. Gloved hands. A gun the size of a cannon. Catching her off guard, he flipped her onto her back, his strength terrifying. She caught a glint of the chrome cuffs, realized he was going to cuff her with her hands in front of her, and slashed at him with her nails. All the while she wondered where Jake was. Why hadn't he come to her aid? Had they hurt him? Or worse?

He caught her wrists. "Let go of me!" she shouted.

Her shout was cut short by a gloved hand slapped over her mouth hard enough to cut her lip. "Shut up."

Leigh fought for her life. She knew if he got those cuffs on her, her fate would be sealed.

A dark shadow rushed them from the side. She heard the sound of something solid slamming into flesh. The man grunted, but the sound was cut short when a booted foot landed solidly on the side of his head. His head pitched violently back. A final kick sent the man sprawling into the snow.

Strong hands reached for her. She scrambled away, got to her hands and knees, tried to get her feet under her.

"Jake!" She shouted his name when the hands closed over her shoulders.

"Leigh. It's me. Calm down."

Jake.

"You're safe," he said.

Still shaking, she looked over to see Jake cuffing the man's hands behind him. But his eyes were on her. "Are you all right?" he asked.

"You mean aside from a near heart attack?"

Rising, he offered his hand. "There are more where he came from," he said, looking down at the man lying cuffed on the ground. "We need to leave. Now."

The next thing she knew he was pulling her to her feet and into a dead run toward the truck. Leigh couldn't stop looking over her shoulder. How could Rasmussen possibly have known where to find them?

At the truck Jake opened her door and shoved her inside. "Get on the floor. Don't argue."

Leigh slid from the seat and knelt on the floorboard, her heart hammering like a piston against her ribs. Jake slid behind the wheel and started the engine. He didn't turn on the lights as he started down the lane.

"What the hell were you doing outside?" he asked.

"I...I needed to use the facilities. He came at me out of nowhere." A shudder moved through her when she remembered how easily the man had overpowered her. "How did you know?"

"You shouting your head off was a dead giveaway."

Leigh shook her head. "How did they find us?"

"They've been tracking us all along."

"What?"

"They're using a high-tech GPS device deployed via a special bullet designed to withstand high impact and attach itself to the target."

"My God." She listened, fear vibrating through her as he explained how the miniature GPS transmitters worked. "How did you figure that out?"

"I called a friend."

"A friend at MIDNIGHT?"

"Zack Devlin knows electronics."

"Does that mean Mike Madrid didn't give us up?"

Jake grimaced. "Probably."

She thought about that a moment. "Is Rasmussen still able to track us?"

"I removed all the transmitters I could find." He sent her a dark look. "Let's just hope I didn't miss one."

Sliding onto the seat, she pressed her hand

against her stomach, feeling sick. "I thought they had hurt you. I thought they had—"

"They didn't," he said. "Don't even go there."

Fighting back tears, Leigh looked out at the vast darkness. What would she have done back there without Jake? "You saved my life," she said.

"I did what I had to do to get us out of there."

When she had her emotions under control, she turned to face him. "Rasmussen is not going to stop. He's evil and obsessed and seems to have every resource at his fingertips."

"Every federal and state law enforcement agency within a five-hundred-mile radius is looking for him, Leigh."

"He's too smart to get caught, Jake. You know that as well as I do."

His jaw flexed. "He may be smart, but he's not invincible."

"Money and connections buy an awful lot of invincible."

"Sooner or later his obsession with you will get the best of him. He'll make a mis-

take. When he does, I'm going to make damn
sure I'm there to take him down."

As the dark landscape whizzed by, all
Leigh could think was that she hoped they
lived long enough to do just that.

AFTER THE AMBUSH back at the grain elevator, Jake hadn't been able to take his eyes off
the rearview mirror, certain he'd missed at
least one of the GPS transmitters that had
penetrated the body of the truck. But as the
night wore on and Rasmussen's thugs didn't
show, he began to think that perhaps he'd
gotten them all.

He was working on forty-eight hours
without sleep, and by noon he was feeling
every minute of fatigue. They needed a place
to rest and eat and sleep. Damn it, Leigh
was right. They needed a plan. Desperate
and exhausted, he decided to take her to the
only place he could think of.

He hadn't been to the Thunder Cove Marina for almost two months. It had been even
longer since he'd sailed. But he'd kept the
Stormy C. in the water, just in case.

It was nearly dusk and snowing in earnest

when he parked the truck in a spot hidden from the street. On the seat next to him, Leigh thrashed in her sleep. She'd done that a lot since leaving the grain elevator. Jake set his hand on her shoulder. "Leigh."

She sat up abruptly, her eyes wide with fear. Then she blinked at him, pulled herself together.

"You're all right." He touched her arm and was surprised to feel her trembling. "It was just a bad dream."

Even tousled, exhausted and scared, she was beautiful.

"I can't believe I fell asleep." She looked around. "Where are we?"

"Thunder Cove," he said.

"I have no idea where that is."

"Lake Michigan. I keep my sailboat here."

"A little cold for sailing, isn't it?"

He smiled. "Yeah, but the boat will be warm inside."

"Looks deserted."

"Not many people out this time of year. Nobody knows I keep a boat here. We can eat, grab a shower, get some sleep." He could sure as hell use all those things. "Maybe afterward we can come up with some kind of plan."

When she didn't say anything he reached out and stroked her cheek with the backs of his fingers. "You okay?"

She nodded. "Just a little jumpy."

"Bullets tend to do that to a person."

It was her turn to smile, but he didn't miss the shadows in her eyes. He wished he could take those shadows away. He wished even more fervently that the circumstances were different.

Sighing, Jake opened the door. The frigid wind coming off the lake struck him like a glass of ice water. He went to open Leigh's door, but she was already sliding to the ground. He motioned toward the chain-link gate and the marina beyond.

"I didn't know you had a boat," she said as they headed toward the gate.

"I don't sail much anymore."

"Why not?"

"Never make time." Jake used his key and opened the gate.

"There aren't many boats in the water."

"Most people store their vessels in dry

dock during the winter season. Ice can damage the hulls."

"You don't have yours stored?"

"I haven't had it taken out of the water yet this year."

"What about the ice?"

"I have what's called a bubble system installed. Keeps the water surrounding the hull from freezing."

They started down the wooden floating dock. The slip where Jake kept the *Stormy C.* was located at the end of the second row. She was a sleek twenty-eight-foot Beneteau 285 he'd bought used three years earlier. He'd always dreamed of owning a sailboat. Now that he had one, the job kept him so busy he rarely sailed.

Jake stepped onto the deck and offered his hand to Leigh. "Be careful. It's slick."

She accepted his hand and followed. "Looks like we're in for more snow."

"Lake effect," he said. "Welcome to Michigan in November."

Her hand was like ice within his. He found himself not wanting to let it go. Not now. Not ever. But Jake didn't have the luxury of indulging in the pleasure of holding her hand. Not when there was a killer with both of them in his sights.

Tugging the flashlight from his coat pocket, he unlocked the hatch and lifted the dual doors. The nautical odors of mildew and damp teak greeted him as he descended the companionway steps. He checked the forward and aft berths and the head. When he was satisfied they were alone, he went back on deck to the cockpit, turned on the bilge blower and started the diesel engine.

Leigh was sitting on the galley settee when he returned. Jake thought he'd never seen any-one look as tired as she did at that moment. Her shoulders were slumped. Her head hung slightly. He figured he didn't look much better.

"Heat should start pumping in a few minutes," he said. "Ten minutes and we'll have hot water."

"This boat has a shower?" She perked up.

He motioned toward the head. "It's small but functional." He then reached into his coat pocket for his pistol. "There's a restaurant in town a few miles from here."

"I'm starved..." Her voice trailed when she spotted the gun.

Jake pressed it into her hand. "I'm going to lock the door behind me. You'll be safe here. But just in case, I want you to keep this with you. Take it into the shower. Take it to bed. But be prepared to use it if you have to. You got that?"

"What about you?"

He patted the pistol he'd lifted from the thug back at the grain elevator. "I've got this one in case I need it."

He prayed he wasn't going to need it.

LEIGH DIDN'T THINK she was ever going to be warm again. She huddled beneath the hot spray of the shower in the tiny head of Jake's sailboat until the water ran cold. When she shut down the faucets, she heard Jake moving around in the galley.

She'd been trying not to think about the kiss they'd shared back at the grain elevator. But her mind—not to mention her body— would not let her forget it. Intellectually she knew Ian Rasmussen presented a much bigger problem. She should be thinking of ways to stay out of his grasp. Instead she kept thinking about how it had felt when Jake's mouth had been pressed against hers....

Exasperated with herself, she quickly toweled herself dry. She was loath to put on the same clothes, but with nothing else to wear she didn't have a choice.

The aroma of something warm and delicious titillated her nose when she opened the door. Jake was in the galley with his back to her. Then he turned and she noticed the bottle of wine in one hand, two plastic wineglasses in the other.

For a second he looked sheepish. Then a slow smile tugged at his mouth, and she felt something begin to melt inside her.

"I figured we could both use a little down time," he said.

Leigh didn't know what to say. Down time was one thing. Sharing a bottle of wine with a man whose smile could melt even the most steadfast of female resolves—a man she was wildly attracted to—was quite another.

"It's French," he added. As if that mattered. "Merlot. I hope that's all right."

"Oh. Um." It was as intelligent an answer as she could muster at the moment.

"How's the bullet wound?" he asked.

She stared, her heart beating just a little too fast as he set the glasses on the table and poured. "Fine."

"Warm enough for you?"

Hot, she thought dazedly, then realized that would not be an appropriate response and shrugged. "It's fine."

"I bought soup." He motioned to the tiny stovetop burner in the galley. "If you'll keep an eye on it, I'd like to grab a quick shower." He handed her a glass of wine.

Leigh accepted the wine, hoping he didn't notice that her hand was trembling.

"We're safe here," he said, obviously misunderstanding the source of her nervousness.

She sipped the wine, found it deep and smoky with a hint of berry. Jake stepped close to her. She was about to step back when his hands went to the buttons on his shirt. Leigh's face heated as he unbuttoned them. Never taking his eyes from hers, he eased the shirt from his shoulders.

It had been six years since she'd seen Jake

Vanderpol's naked chest. But she'd never forgotten the magnificence of it. His shoulders were as hard and wide as boulders. His pectoral muscles were well defined, his biceps rounded with muscle. A thatch of black hair covered his chest, tapering onto his washboard abs.

Suddenly the cabin seemed too small for both of them. Leigh knew it was stupid, but she wanted to bolt, even though she fully realized this man had done nothing but protect her in the days they'd been together. Still she needed to get away from the knowing glint in his eyes. From the stark temptation of the body she'd never been able to get out of her system.

"I'll watch the soup," she blurted.

One side of his mouth hiked into a smile. "Don't let it boil."

When her face heated, he smiled and said, "The burner is temperamental. Gets too hot for comfort sometimes."

All she could think was that when it came to Jake Vanderpol the stove wasn't the only thing that got too hot for comfort.

Chapter Twelve

Leigh stirred the soup, but her mind was elsewhere. Four feet away to be exact. As much as she'd tried to keep her relationship with Jake impersonal—as fervently as she tried not to let the past get in the way of the present—she couldn't stop herself from picturing him beneath the spray of the shower, his hands soaping the hard planes of the most magnificent male body she'd ever seen. She imagined those same callused male hands, slicked with soap and running over her own body.

"Soup's about to boil over."

She started at the sound of Jake's voice right behind her. She looked down at the pan and sure enough the soup was boiling into froth.

"Damn," she muttered.

Jake nudged her aside and expertly adjusted the burner. Leigh didn't know why she was such a wreck. It wasn't as if she was going to act on any of the impulses streaking through her brain. Jake had hurt her badly the last time she'd opened up to him. It had taken her a long time to get to the place where she was now.

She busied herself setting the table while Jake ladled soup into bowls. "I bought this from the diner in town," he said.

It was the best soup Leigh had ever tasted. She didn't realize how hungry she was until her bowl was empty and Jake was ladling more into it. The wine had settled her nerves, and she knew she couldn't put off any longer what she'd been dreading.

"We need to find a way to stop Rasmussen," she began. "We're not going to be able to hide out here forever."

"I checked in with Cutter when I drove into town."

"What did he say?"

"They think Rasmussen has left the country."

Leigh wanted to believe that, but she didn't. She'd lived with Rasmussen for over a year; a fact that invariably shamed her. She knew he wasn't the kind of man who gave up so easily. "Do you believe that?"

Jake's gaze met hers. "Possibly. But if he has, he hasn't gone far. Canada probably, where he's still close enough to oversee his thugs and hunt for us."

She swirled the soup with her spoon, her appetite waning. "Is MIDNIGHT going to continue searching for him?"

"Yes, but manpower is stretched thin. Agents in multiple federal agencies, multiple jurisdictions are scrambling due to the Witness Security Program being hacked."

The thought of hundreds of terrified witnesses—some of them with families and children—under threat by different factions of organized crime sickened her. "Apprehending him isn't a priority."

"It is. But protecting those witnesses comes first. Cutter doesn't have the kind of manpower he needs to get Rasmussen as quickly as I'd like."

"Does that mean we're on our own?"

"That means we need to lay low for a while."

"I've been laying low for six years, Jake." Restless and frustrated, Leigh rose and paced to the small window. The marina was quiet and deserted. Snow continued to fall. The scene should have been peaceful, but it wasn't. "I'm tired of always having to look over my shoulder."

"I know it's been hard," he said.

"I want my life back."

She heard Jake rise. She tensed when he came over to her side and put his hands on her shoulders. How easy it would be to turn to him and take refuge in the strength of his arms. But after Rasmussen—after Jake— Leigh had promised herself no more mistakes.

She relaxed marginally when he handed her the glass of wine she'd left on the table. "I know it's hard, but try to be patient," he said.

"I'm tired of being patient. Of running scared. I'm tired of having to move every few months." She turned to him, set the wine on the table. "We have to stop him."

"We don't have the resources at the moment."

"There has to be a way."

"I'm not going to risk getting you killed, Leigh. Obsession, jealousy and hatred are ugly emotions. Think about it. A sane man would have cut his losses and run as far away as he could."

"Maybe we can find his weak spot. Use it to—"

"Damn it, Leigh, let me handle this."

"I deserve to have my life back, Jake. Don't take that away from me."

"I'm not going to let you get yourself hurt."

"I'm not some bumbling idiot. Damn it, I know Rasmussen. I know how he thinks."

"Then you know he doesn't have a conscience!" Jake shouted abruptly.

"I know stopping him is my only hope of ever having a normal life! Of having a future!"

Jake grasped her arms. "I'm not going to let him kill you!"

Leigh stared into his furious eyes, and realized fury was not the only emotion he was feeling. Jake Vanderpol was also frightened.

"You're afraid of him," she said.

His jaw flexed. "You're damn right I'm scared! I know what he'll do to you if he gets his hands on you. I've seen his handiwork, Leigh, and it's brutal. If you weren't so damn stubborn, you'd be afraid, too."

Leigh was a hell of a lot more than afraid. She was terrified of Rasmussen. But she'd been running for too long. "If I don't stop him, I'm giving up my life. Hiding in the shadows. Never having a future. You can't expect me to do that."

"The one thing I do expect is for you to be alive every single day for the rest of my life."

"Why do you care?" she asked with sudden anger. "I'll be living in some town so small it won't even make the map. You won't be there—"

"I care about you!" he roared. "Why can't you get that through your head!"

The words struck her like a fist. Too stunned to react, she continued staring into his blazing eyes, seeing more than she wanted to see, feeling more than she wanted to feel. She spun away from him and fled, knowing she was dangerously close to mak-

ing a mistake that would only bring her heart-
ache. She heard her name behind her as she
climbed up the companionway and through
the hatch, but she didn't stop.

Snow swirled down from a black sky. She
could hear the water slapping against the
pier, the boat rigging clanging against the
poles in a brisk northerly wind. She heard
Jake behind her, but she didn't turn around
to face him. She didn't want him to see what
she knew her face would reveal.

"Leigh, come back below."

When she didn't move, he went to her.
He turned her toward him.

"It's cold," he said. "You're shivering."

The tremors ripping through her body had
nothing to do with the cold and everything to
do with the man.

"You know I'm right," she said.

"I know you've got some very dangerous
ideas floating around inside that head of
yours."

"Don't tell me you wouldn't be thinking
the very same thing."

"I probably would." He sighed. "But I
damn well don't like it.

"I don't like any of this."

She saw snowflakes in his hair. Clinging to his lashes. He was staring at her mouth, and she knew what would happen next. She could feel the emotions winding up inside her. The physical sensations swamping her with heat.

"I can't stand the thought of you getting hurt," he said roughly.

"I know it's risky," she said. "But what is the alternative? Give up my future so I can be safe? What kind of life is that?"

Cursing beneath his breath, he pulled her to him. Her legs went weak when he kissed her. He tasted like wine and frustration and restraint. When he pulled away, his jaw was taut. "I think I have a plan that might work," he said, motioning toward the hatch. "Let's go below and I'll fill you in."

IAN RASMUSSEN was accustomed to getting his way. It didn't go over well when Derrick LeValley came to his suite and told him about the GPS transmitters.

"How could he possibly have known about the transmitters?" Rasmussen asked.

"I don't know. It's possible he is an electronics expert. Or he could have been in touch with one of the agents at MID-NIGHT."

Rasmussen almost smiled when he thought of the federal agency that, six years ago, had brought down the empire he'd worked so hard to build. No doubt their agents were scrambling as they assisted the U.S. Marshals Service to get all of their precious witnesses covered. The small success tasted like the sweetest of chocolates. But it wasn't enough. He wanted Kelsey. And he wanted Vanderpol dead. Until both of those things were done, he would never be able to rest.

Sighing in annoyance, Rasmussen crossed to the bar and poured himself two fingers of cognac. "Where are they?"

"We don't exactly know." LeValley cleared his throat. "Somewhere in southern Michigan."

LeValley's anxiety pleased him. "How do you plan to find them?"

"I've got people working on deep background checks. Family members. Friends. Property they own. Something will pop."

"I don't need to remind you that our Canadian friends will only be able to conceal me for so long, do I?"

"Sir, I know you don't want to leave the country without her, but for your own safety—"

"*Safety?*" Rasmussen threw his head back and laughed.

LeValley watched him warily.

"Don't tell me about goddamn safety. I want her. I want her now. And I want Vanderpol. I'm going to kill him myself, and I can tell you it's going to take some time."

"Yes, sir." LeValley swallowed hard. "I've got a container ship that is in the process of being renovated. It has a hidden compartment with first-class living quarters. It will get you down the St. Lawrence River, through the locks. From there you'll be shipped to Cuba where the Lear will be waiting to take you to Morocco."

That would give him *days* to mete out his revenge on Vanderpol. Days to hear the other man's screams. Days for Kelsey to hear them. And all the while she would be in his bed where she belonged....

Rasmussen looked at the gold Rolex strapped to his wrist. "You have two hours to find them."

"Two hours?" LeValley choked out a sound. "But that's not enough time."

"I suggest you get started. If you do not locate them, the consequences will be severe. Are we clear?"

"Yes, sir," he said and started for the door at a brisk clip.

Sipping the cognac, Rasmussen watched him leave. When the glass was empty, he hurled it into the brick hearth. "I'm coming for you, Kelsey," he whispered.

And hatred burned from the depths of his heart.

JAKE DIDN'T LIKE the plan one iota. To even consider using Leigh as bait filled him with deep, dark dread. But of all the strategies he'd considered in the last days, the one he was about to lay out for her seemed the safest route to take…if there was a safe route when it came to a madman like Rasmussen.

He folded the table where they'd eaten, then slid onto the settee. He watched Leigh pour two glasses of wine and tried hard not to notice that her hands were shaking. *So much for the bravado,* he thought. The woman was terrified. Truth be told, so was he.

Handing him the glass of wine, she slid onto the settee, a safe distance away. "Tell me about this plan of yours."

Jake accepted the wine and set it on the table in front of him without drinking. "The last time we needed Rasmussen to bite, you were the bait."

Her gaze didn't waiver. "I didn't like the way it went down, Jake, but it was an effective plan."

"Before I get into this, I want you to understand that I won't do that to you again, Leigh. I won't use you. I won't risk your getting hurt."

"Jake—"

"Hear me out." He raised a hand to silence her. "A good friend of mine, Ronald Waite, is a reporter for a tabloid based in Chicago, the *Investigator.* Four years ago, while he was in Mexico, his little boy was kidnapped and held for ransom. The MIDNIGHT Agency was called in. I was assigned the case. To make a long story short, I got his kid back. Ronald has kept in touch, and he ends every e-mail, every phone call with 'if there's ever anything I can do for you.'"

"How can a reporter help us?" Leigh asked.

"Sometimes law enforcement agencies use the media as a tool to bring about an arrest. The media can plant information. Withhold information. In this case, Ronald has been reporting on Rasmussen's escape since it happened. I could ask him to reveal a bogus location where you're allegedly hiding out. A location that in reality you won't be anywhere near. When Rasmussen shows, he'll get the surprise of his life because I'll be the one waiting for him."

LEIGH DIDN'T LIKE the plan. There were too many variables. Too many things that could go wrong. But for the life of her she couldn't come up with anything better.

She gazed at Jake, and all she could think was that if Rasmussen got the chance, he would kill him.

"I'm not the only one he wants dead," she said.

"I'm a trained agent."

"Who just happens to have walked off the job—"

"If Rasmussen comes after me he will have bitten off more than he can chew."

"You no longer have the resources of the agency to come in and back you up if something goes wrong." She knew that when it came to Rasmussen, something always went wrong.

"You have a better idea?"

She wished she did. "With some time maybe we could come up with something—"

"We're out of time, Leigh. In just two days, both of us have had close encounters with bullets. You've seen the lengths to which he will go. You've seen the technology he has. You know what he's capable of."

"Jake, I don't want you hurt."

An emotion she couldn't quite identify flickered in his eyes, but it was gone so quickly she didn't have time to examine it. "I'm going to call Ronald," he said. "He'll probably have to get this okayed by his editor. But he may be able to get something in the *Investigator* tomorrow."

Unclipping his cell phone from his belt, he rose. Before even realizing she was going to move, her hand snaked out, her fingers wrapped around his arm. "Are you sure about this?" she asked.

"I want him off the street before he hurts even more people."

Standing on tiptoe, she leaned close and pressed a chaste kiss to his cheek. "Thank you for being so willing to put yourself on the line for me."

"You did it for us six years ago," he said.

Her face was only a few inches from his. She could see the dark shadow of two-day-old whiskers. Feeling a swirl of dizziness, she stepped back.

For a moment his gaze searched hers.

Then without another word he turned and headed up the companionway, dialing his phone as he went.

Chapter Thirteen

Ronald Waite arrived at nine o'clock sharp. "Ahoy!"

Leigh had just made coffee when she heard the greeting. Six years of being in hiding had made her skittish when it came to strangers. But one look at the grin on Jake's face as he started toward the companionway, and she knew the man who'd approached the boat was a friend.

In the galley she set coffee and cups on the table. Up on deck she could hear the men talking and laughing and she slowly began to relax. A few minutes later the two men descended the companionway.

"You didn't tell me she was beautiful." Smiling, Ronald Waite stuck out his hand.

Leigh couldn't help it—she smiled back

as she took his hand. "Thanks for coming," she said.

With a head of bright-red hair and a ruddy face covered with freckles, the reporter was not what she'd expected. He wore a blue parka with a faux-fur collar. She guessed his age to be about forty.

Five minutes later they were seated at the table with bagels and steaming cups of coffee.

"You're staying here on the boat?" Ronald asked.

"For now," Jake said. "I don't want to stay at any one place too long."

"I've been thinking about this plan of yours." Ronald sipped his coffee. "I think it will work."

"Logistics might be a problem," Jake said.

"And whether or not Rasmussen will bite," Leigh added.

Ronald reached across the table and patted her hand. "He'll bite, honey. Trust me."

"I need a remote location for a meet," Jake said. He looked at Waite. "What I need from you is to reveal Leigh's alleged location. That's where Rasmussen will show. And that's where I'll be waiting for him."

Waite helped himself to a bagel. "I can help you with both. I've got a cabin a hundred miles north of here, in the Upper Peninsula. I take my wife and kids up there a couple of times a year. My brother-in-law has a cabin just across the lake from ours, about three miles away."

"Remote?" Jake asked. "I don't want any civilians around."

"No neighbors for miles. The closest sign of civilization is a gas station ten miles away."

Jake nodded and glanced at Leigh. "Here's how we'll work it. We stash you in the cabin across the lake." He looked at Waite. "I'll hole up in your cabin. You reveal Leigh's location in the *Investigator.* Don't make it too easy for Rasmussen. Give just enough information for him to figure things out."

Leigh didn't like the way Jake was laying this out. There were so many things that could go wrong. "Jake, you're talking about going to a remote location and taking on a violent man who has a small army to back him up. You can't do this completely on your own. You're going to need support in case something goes wrong."

"I've got a friend I can call," he said.

"Who?"

He stared at her, saying nothing.

"One of the agents from MIDNIGHT?"

Jake turned his attention back to Ronald Waite. "How quickly can you put this story together?"

"I already obtained permission from the city desk manager. I can write it this afternoon when I get back and have it into tomorrow's edition."

RONALD WAITE DEPARTED fifteen minutes later, leaving a map and directions to both cabins with Jake. By noon Jake and Leigh were back in the truck and on the road heading north into Michigan's upper peninsula.

Forced to stick to the back roads, they arrived at the cabin at dusk. Leigh found the scene to be as picturesque as any she had ever seen. A log cabin nestled in the woods, the boughs of the firs and spruces heavy with snow. The cabin had a river rock chimney jutting into a slate-gray sky.

"Nice place," Leigh commented.

He unlocked the door and they walked inside.

The interior was rustic and beautiful. The pine plank floor in the living room was covered with a Navajo rug. The furniture was bold with a Southwestern flair. There were two bedrooms, a full bathroom with a heated tile floor, and two cords of wood were stacked on the back porch.

Within minutes Jake had a fire blazing in the hearth. Because she needed something to do, Leigh made coffee in the kitchen, then joined Jake in front of the fire.

She handed him a steaming mug. "Do you think the plan is going to work?"

He took the coffee and sipped, watching her over the rim. "Rasmussen will jump at any chance to get to you."

She withheld the shudder that threatened. "What if he doesn't read the story?"

"The *Investigator* is widely read. We'll give him a few days. Ron is going to run the story online, as well. Even if Rasmussen doesn't read it, someone he knows will probably tell him about the story. I know from the months I hunted him that he's an information junkie." Jake shrugged. "If he doesn't bite the first day, I'll have Ronald run a different story, citing the same location a second time."

"Ian is smart, Jake. What if he realizes it's a trap?"

"Ronald is a good writer. He'll reveal just enough information for Rasmussen to figure out the location. He won't make it too easy for him."

Leigh was tired, but her mind was wound tight. Unable to sit, she began to pace, going through the gauntlet of all the things that could go wrong.

Jake came up behind her and set his hands on her shoulders. "You wear a hole in that rug and we're going to have some explaining to do to Ronald's brother-in-law," he said.

She choked out a laugh and turned to face him. "I'm worried. Pacing is what nervous people do."

"I'm not going to tell you this isn't dangerous. But I will tell you that I'm not going to let anything go wrong. I'm sure as hell not going to let Rasmussen get to you. Do you understand?"

"It's not me I'm worried about, Jake. It's

you. Rasmussen is insanely jealous. He knows that you and I..." Because she didn't know quite how to finish the sentence she sighed. "He knows we were together. He's not going to let that go."

"I can handle him, Leigh. Give me some credit. I'm a trained agent. I know firearms. And I've seen Rasmussen's psychological profile. I'm quite aware of what he's capable of."

"He's a monster," she whispered.

"He's only a man. A man with weaknesses just like everyone else. I know he's going to bite. And I know this plan is the best way to smoke him out of his hole so we can end this." He squeezed her shoulders. "So you can get your life back."

The thought bolstered her, but it was only a tiny light at the end of a long, dark and very dangerous tunnel. For the first time since the nightmare had begun, she was more afraid for Jake than she was for herself.

"I can barely imagine what it would be like not to have to look over my shoulder every minute of every day."

"Once he's in custody, MIDNIGHT will

work in conjunction with other law enforcement agencies to dismantle the remainder of his organization. Once that happens, neither will be a threat to you any longer. Try to keep that in mind, Leigh."

Standing there looking into Jake's dark eyes, feeling his strong hands on her shoulders, she almost believed everything was going to be all right.

She jolted when a particularly hard gust of wind shook the cabin.

"Just the wind," he said softly.

Embarrassed, Leigh laughed. "I'm jumping at shadows."

"We're safe until that story runs." Raising his hand, he brushed a stray hair from her cheek. "You're safe with me."

The moment had become intimate. Leigh was trembling, but it wasn't from fear. It was because of Jake. The way he was looking at her. The way he was touching her. The way her body was responding.

She had vowed she would not let down her guard. That she would not give in to the demands of her body when it came to Jake Vanderpol. But when he dipped his head and brushed his mouth against hers, Leigh forgot all about the promises she'd made to herself and kissed him back.

When he ran his hands over her shoulders and down her back, shivers of delight cascaded through her body.

"Come here," he whispered.

He didn't wait for her to comply and pulled her against him. His body was like sculpted steel against hers. Leigh fit perfectly. Too perfectly, she thought dazedly.

Then he was kissing her and she couldn't think of anything at all. Hot, demanding kisses that scattered her thoughts and tore down her resistance. Jake was the only man who'd ever been able to make her forget about right and wrong.

She didn't make a conscious decision to kiss him back, but the next thing she knew she was clinging to him. Her mouth was on his, demanding more, and he was sliding his tongue into her as if she were an elixir and he an addict for it. She could feel the hard ridge of his erection against her pelvis.

He lifted her sweater. She raised her arms and he eased it over her head so that she was wearing nothing but her bra and jeans. A shudder went through her when he pulled back and looked at her. A shudder that had nothing to do with the chill inside the cabin and everything to do with the heat zinging between them.

"You're so beautiful."

He caressed her with his eyes, and Leigh felt as if he'd run his fingertips over her with a feather touch.

Never taking his eyes from hers, he unclasped her bra. She shivered when he removed the scrap of lace from her shoulders.

"I missed you," he said. "For six years I've never stopped thinking of you, never stopped worrying about you, or hating myself for the way things went down."

Taking her face between his hands, he forced her gaze to his. "I'm sorry," he said. "I'm sorry I did what I did. I'm sorry Rasmussen hurt you. I'm sorry I hurt you."

Unexpected tears stung her eyes. "I believe you," she whispered.

"I will never let him hurt you again. I'll never put you in harm's way. You have my word on that."

He kissed her then. A long, lingering kiss that shot sparks throughout her body. He trailed kisses down her throat. Bending slightly, he kissed the valley between her breasts.

Leigh moaned when he took her nipple into his mouth. Her body arched, offering him more. Jake took it, laving his tongue over her swollen nipple. The arousal pulsing between her legs turned fierce.

The ringing of a cell phone came to her as if from a long distance. Jake pulled away, strode quickly to his phone and snatched it up. "Vanderpol."

As he listened, his mouth formed a thin line. Then the blood drained from his face, and Leigh suddenly knew who was on the other end of the line. But how had he gotten Jake's number?

"THERE WAS A DREADFUL incident at the Thunder Cove Marina this afternoon," Rasmussen said. "An explosion and fire, I'm told. A nice sailboat, the *Stormy C.,* I believe, went up in flames. Very unfortunate."

Jake knew the sailboat could be replaced.

But that didn't keep the burst of rage from spreading through him like fire. "I'm sure you had nothing to do with it."

"Had we been a few hours earlier, you and Kelsey might have been inside. Or is she going by Leigh these days?"

"It doesn't matter, because as long as I'm alive you'll never see her again."

"Rest assured, Mr. Vanderpol. I'll see her again. I'll do a lot more than just see her. I'll have her. I'll taste her. I'll see you again, too."

A nasty curse flew from Jake's mouth. He hit End, then stood there, his pulse hammering.

"Jake? What is it?"

Leigh's voice came to him as if from a great distance.

Forcing his dark emotions back, he locked his gaze to hers. Even furious and afraid, he was taken aback by her beauty. By the effect she had on him.

"Rasmussen," he spat.

She closed the distance between them. He could feel her eyes on him, but he didn't reveal what he was thinking, what he was feeling. She set her hand on his arm.

"My God," she said. "You're shaking. What did he say to you?"

Jake didn't like being afraid. He didn't like knowing an evil man like Rasmussen was out there with his sights set on a woman he cared for. He liked even less the anxious feeling that the other man might succeed.

"The bastard torched the boat," he ground out.

"Oh, Jake. Oh no. I'm sorry."

"It's only a boat, Leigh. It can be replaced. I'm insured."

"But that kind of destruction is so senseless. And I know how much you loved that boat."

All Jake could think was that his feelings for her were a hell of a lot more powerful. "I don't know how he found out about it. Nobody knew about the boat. Not even the people at MIDNIGHT." But he knew the folks at MIDNIGHT had ways of finding out just about anything. Once again he got the uneasy feeling that someone at MIDNIGHT had given him up. But who?

"Jake, this drives home the point that we need to trap him. Sooner or later Rasmussen is going to catch up with us. I'd rather that happen on our terms instead of his."

Looking into the deep blue of her eyes he wanted desperately to argue. But logic wouldn't let him. She was right. They needed to trap Rasmussen to stop him. But was stopping a madman worth risking her life? "I know," he said. "We made the right decision."

But suddenly Jake began to doubt his ability to keep her safe. He'd been considering calling Sean Cutter and asking the agency for support. But after everything that happened, Jake wasn't sure he could trust the agency. If someone inside was selling information, both he and Leigh were as good as dead. No, he thought darkly. They were on their own.

"We carry out the sting as planned," he said.

She nodded.

The need to reach out to her was strong, but Jake resisted. He knew what would happen if he did.

"We ought to try to get some sleep," he said in a rough voice. "I'll take the rear bedroom. You can have the master."

She started to speak, but Jake turned and walked into the bedroom.

Chapter Fourteen

Jake didn't know what he was afraid of, but the fear was like a living creature inside him. A creature panicked and running for its life. Certain of death.

Then he saw Leigh. Wearing nothing more than a gauzy gown, she ran toward him through the thick, dark forest. The whirling snow came up to her knees but it didn't slow her down. He sensed her panic. He saw the terror on her face. He didn't know what she was running from. But he sensed evil. He felt it all the way to his bones.

"Jake!" she shouted as she ran. "Help me, please!"

He wanted to go to her, wrap her in his arms and keep her safe. But he was paralyzed; he

couldn't move. "Leigh! I'm here!" he shouted.
"Run!"

But she couldn't hear him above the keening of the wind.

Then Ian Rasmussen appeared out of nowhere, wearing a black tuxedo and armed with a long barrel rifle. Rasmussen raised the rifle and took aim.

Arms outstretched, Leigh cried out for Jake to help her.

"Leigh!" Jake yelled.

The gunshot shattered the night. Jake watched as red bloomed on the front of her gown. She stopped running and set her hand against the wound. Her eyes were accusing when they fell upon Jake.

"You used me," she whispered. "You betrayed me."

"No!" he shouted.

But when he looked down at his own hands, they were covered with blood.

"No!"

Jake sat bolt upright, his heart hammering like a piston. Sweat slicked his body.

The image of Leigh being shot made him

physically ill. The fear was like a stone in his gut.

Throwing his legs over the side of the bed, he rose.

"Jake?"

He started at the sound of her voice. Glancing quickly toward the door, he noticed her standing there.

"What are you doing in here?" he asked, his voice sounding more rough than he'd intended.

"You cried out in your sleep. I wanted to make sure you were all right."

"I'm fine."

Evidently, she didn't believe him because she went to him. Annoyed by her concern, Jake sighed heavily. "Damn it, Leigh, I'm fine."

But he started when she touched his arm.

"My God, you're wet with sweat."

She moved closer as if to set her palm against his forehead to check for a fever, but he stopped her by grasping her wrist. "I said I'm all right." He released her a little too roughly.

"You're not sick?"

"No."

She eyed him as if she didn't know whether to believe him. "Did you have a nightmare?"

"It was just a stupid dream." He scraped a hand over his face, wished he hadn't when he noticed it was shaking.

"What was it about?"

He didn't want to talk about the dream. He could recall the stark terror he'd felt when Rasmussen shot her down. He could still see her face, the shock in her eyes, and feel the horror in his heart. Standing there close enough to touch her, all he could do was pray to God he would never have to face what he'd faced in that nightmare.

Shaken by the thought, torn because he wanted to be with her in ways that would only complicate a situation that was already too complex, he shoved past her and walked into the living room. The fire in the hearth had burned down to embers. Because he needed something to do, he put two more logs on the grate.

"You were in bad shape when I walked into the bedroom."

He turned to find her standing directly behind him. "It was just a bad dream, Leigh. Let it go."

"A bad dream that had you sweating and shaking as if you were deathly ill. For God's sake, you're *still* shaking."

"Yeah, well, it's freaking cold in here."

"Sometimes it helps to talk things out."

He wished she would stop looking at him like that. As if he was the only man in the world and all the things that had happened six years ago no longer mattered.

Then he noticed she was only wearing a T-shirt and a pair of socks. Her legs were bare, and he couldn't take his eyes off that tantalizing stretch of skin. Then he remembered he was wearing only his boxer shorts and a T-shirt and if he didn't get the hell out of there pronto she was going to know exactly how much he liked looking at her.

"Go back to bed," he said gruffly.

Neither of them moved, and Jake knew his fate was sealed. He went to her in two resolute strides. She took a single step back. A gasp escaped her when his fingers closed around her arms. Then his mouth came down on hers and he couldn't think of anything except the pleasure raging through his body.

"I can't bear the thought of you getting hurt," he whispered.

"I'm not going to get hurt."

"I'm not going to let him hurt you."

He knew he was reacting to the nightmare. But there were other emotions involved. His attraction to her was tearing at his judgment, making him want her when he knew it would be smarter for him to walk away before the situation got too hot.

But the situation was already too hot. Jake felt every sizzling degree. He knew he was going to get burned. But the pleasure of this precious moment would be worth every hour of pain he suffered later.

She tasted as rich and forbidden as sin, and he fed on her like a man deprived. Jake figured that wasn't far from the truth. He'd been deprived since she'd walked out of his life six years ago.

He kissed her until his head spun and his body felt as if it would explode. Pulling away slightly, he looked into her eyes. "I've been wanting to do that to you every single day for six long years."

Her nostrils flared with each labored breath. "We can't go back to the way it was."

"No, but we can move forward." He kissed her again. "The way I see it, I figure we've got some time to make up for."

LEIGH HAD KNOWN this moment would come. She'd thought she'd been prepared for the onslaught of sensation, but nothing could have prepared her for the rush of sheer plea-sure she felt when Jake kissed her.

He was the only man in the world who could sweep her away. Make her forget about right and wrong and consequences. The same thing had happened six years ago when they'd been holed up in that safe house. One touch had led to a kiss. One kiss had ignited a fire that had burned out of con-trol for five days. Five days that had been im-printed on her mind, branded onto her heart, burned into her very soul.

She knew that it was dangerous opening her heart to Jake again, but Leigh was not strong enough to pull away. How could something that felt so right be wrong?

Behind her the fire crackled and popped. Leigh could hear the wind whipping around the cabin. Ice hitting the skylight in the kitchen. She was aware of the warmth of the fire on her back; the hard length of Jake pressed against her; his mouth on hers. One of his hands was at the small of her back, the other cupped the side of her face.

He lifted her up into his arms. She thought he was going to carry her to the bedroom, but instead he lowered her onto the plush rug in front of the fire, then lay down beside her.

Leigh was not totally inexperienced when it came to lovemaking. But Jake wasn't just any man, and she invariably felt overwhelmed when she was with him. He was sure of himself, made no pretenses when it came to taking what he wanted.

She moaned when his hands closed over her breasts and rubbed his thumbs over her sensitized nipples. Need curled low in her pelvis as her body responded.

"I've missed being with you like this," he said. "All those months of not knowing where you were. It damn near killed me, Leigh."

"You kept an eye on me through your resources at MIDNIGHT."

"I knew you were alive. But that didn't make it any easier. It didn't make me worry any less."

He took her mouth in a kiss that was sexual and raw.

Leigh kissed him back with equal ferocity. Every emotion that had been locked inside her for the past six years came pouring out. The force of her passion for Jake stunned her. Made her realize that she was in over her head. Again.

But Leigh couldn't deny there was something different about Jake tonight—an intensity of emotion that hadn't been there before. In the way he touched her. In the way he looked at her. As if he were trying to keep her from slipping away.

He pulled back so he could look into her eyes. "Leigh, promise me you'll stay with me until this is over. Promise me you'll listen to me."

"I will."

"Promise me you'll trust my judgment," he said. "That you won't take any chances—"

"Jake, you're shaking. What's wrong?"

"I don't want you getting hurt."

"Jake, you're frightening me."

"A little fear is probably a good thing right now," he said. "It'll keep you on your toes. Keep you cautious."

Remembering the dream he'd had, Leigh asked, "Is this about the dream? Is that what has you so spooked?"

"This is about Rasmussen." He scrubbed a hand over his jaw. "I don't believe in premonitions."

The uneasiness in his voice told her otherwise. "What premonition? Jake, talk to me."

He was silent for so long that for a moment she thought he wouldn't respond. Sighing, he put his arm around her and held her tightly against him. "We were in blizzard conditions. You were running through the woods. I could see that you were terrified, but I couldn't get to you. Then Rasmussen appeared. He was carrying a rifle. I knew he was going to shoot, but I couldn't move. It was as if I were paralyzed. He raised the rifle." He blew out a breath. "He shot you. I saw you fall."

His gaze was tortured when it met hers. "When I looked down at my hands, they were covered with your blood."

Leigh didn't believe in premonitions, either, but a chill passed through her at his words. "I'm sorry about the nightmare, but I can tell you nothing like that is going to happen."

"You have nothing to be sorry for." His jaw flexed. "But I do."

She didn't want him to say it. An apology now would bring an element to the moment that she wasn't quite ready to handle. Up until now, Leigh had used the past as an excuse. She'd clung to it as a means with which to protect herself from getting too close to Jake.

Looking into his eyes, she knew the past was no longer an issue between them. The realization that her heart was at risk of breaking again made her feel frighteningly vulnerable.

Then Jake skimmed his hands over her body, and Leigh, for the first time in what seemed like forever, lived only in the moment.

Chapter Fifteen

Leigh woke to the smell of coffee. She reached for Jake, the memory of everything that had happened between them the night before flooding back.

Sitting up, she looked around. The small bedroom was very rustic. The bed was constructed of heavy pine. She smiled when she saw the heavy robe and thick wool socks draped across the foot of the bed. They hadn't been there the night before. Jake had done that for her....

She snuggled into the robe, slipped on the socks and padded from the room. She found Jake in the kitchen, his big hands wrapped around a mug of steaming coffee. He smiled when he saw her, and she didn't miss the flash of heat in his eyes.

"Morning."

She smiled back, hating it that she was feeling a little embarrassed. "Hi."

Rising, he went to the coffeemaker and poured. "No cream."

"Black's fine. Smells fabulous."

Instead of handing her the mug, he bent and kissed her. A possessive kiss that told her in no uncertain terms that she was his. "You smell fabulous," he said.

She kissed him back, her pulse spiking.

He deepened the kiss. "You taste even better."

Oh the counter, a portable fax machine began to hum. Groaning, Jake drew away. Looking into her eyes, he traced a finger down her cheek. "Hold that thought," he said and went to the fax.

"All the comforts of home." Shaking from the power of the kiss, Leigh trailed him to the counter and looked over his shoulder.

The fax was a draft of the story that would appear in the *Investigator.* The afterglow of last night melted away as she began to read.

A King's Fall from Grace

Six years ago Ian Rasmussen was a successful North Michigan Avenue restaurateur. One of the Windy City's most eligible bachelors, he owned a four-thousand-square-feet penthouse on Lakeshore Drive. He drove a cherry-red Ferrari and wore five-thousand-dollar Italian suits. He vacationed in the south of France and owned a villa in Monaco.

Then his girlfriend, Kelsey James, discovered he was selling illegal arms to terrorists. She took the information to the police. Several law enforcement agencies worked together and, using Ms. James as bait, initiated an operation that ultimately brought the Rasmussen empire to its knees. Five months later the thirty-two-year-old billionaire was sentenced to life in prison with no chance of parole. Kelsey James went into hiding.

It should have been the end of a long and sordid story. But three days ago, with the help of Derrick LeValley, a former U.S. Marshal, Rasmussen walked

*away from the Terre Haute Federal
Prison. The FBI and U.S. Marshals
Service has refused to comment on the
case. Some speculate Rasmussen used
his vast monetary resources to flee the
country. The* Investigator, *however, has
learned otherwise from Ms. James, who
is staying at an undisclosed location.
She has agreed to a series of exclusive
interviews with the* Investigator...

The story went on to detail Rasmussen's
crimes, including comments from some of
his cell mates about his six-year stint in
prison.

Leigh shook her head. "How is this going
to help us? It doesn't disclose my location."

"If it were that easy he wouldn't bite,"
Jake said.

"Then how are you going to lure him to
the cabin?"

"We know Rasmussen has the ability to
tap phone lines." Jake set his finger against
the byline at the end of the story. "We're
counting on him to do just that."

"You're going to use his own technology and resources against him."

He nodded. "Read on."

If you have any information about Ian Rasmussen or his whereabouts, please contact the Investigator *at 312-555-1234.*

Jake continued. "Every hour or so, Ronald will have a scripted conversation with his editor in which one of them will reveal the location of the cabin. The second the phone line is tapped, Waite will get an alarm. At that point, we'll know Rasmussen is on his way."

"You're counting on something that may not happen."

"You're forgetting I saw Rasmussen's psychological profile. He's got an obsessive personality. Believe me, he'll bite on this."

"And if he's in Canada, like you said he might be?"

Jake's eyes glittered with an unsettling emotion she couldn't quite identify. "There's no way he's not going to go after you. He's too driven by jealousy and hatred."

That wasn't what Leigh wanted to hear.

"I hate this," she said, so tired of being afraid.

"So do I, but it's our best bet. And remember, I'm not going to be alone. Rick Monteith is going to meet me here. He's going to bring a second agent here to stay with you. Unofficially."

Unofficially meant the two men were working without the blessing of the MIDNIGHT Agency. "Why can't you call the agency and get them involved?"

Jake's jaw flexed. "I walked away from the agency, Leigh."

"You're a good agent, Jake. The best, in fact. You know Sean Cutter will take you back."

"Cutter thinks I'm a loose cannon. He'd never condone this. If I try to do this officially, I lose control of the operation." His gaze burned into hers. "I'm not going to give control to someone else. Not when your life is at stake."

Leigh couldn't shake the feeling that something terrible was going to happen. "I have a bad feeling about this."

"Rasmussen is a bad man. Comes with the territory."

"It's not too late to call it off."

He shook his head. "Sooner or later he'll find you, Leigh. I can't let that happen."

"So you're going to risk your own life?"

"You did it for me six years ago."

"That was different."

"He could have found the wire. If he had, we both know he would have killed you."

Shivering, Leigh turned away from him. "I know this sounds crazy, but in his own twisted way, Rasmussen cared for me. But he hates you, Jake."

"I can handle Rasmussen."

She spun to face him. "He'll kill you. I can't bear the thought, Jake. I can't let you do this."

JAKE HATED SEEING HER so afraid. But he had to do this. This was their only chance of stopping Rasmussen. "If we let Rasmussen get away, both of us will be looking over our shoulders for the rest of our lives."

"So we go into hiding."

He grasped her arms. "He'll find you,

Leigh. He'll kill you. He'll kill your friends and family and anyone else who gets in his way. I don't like it any more than you do, but I'm going to do this."

She stared at him, her eyes wide. He could feel her trembling and he hated it. But to give up now would mean she would have to be afraid for the rest of her life. She would be in danger the rest of her life. He knew Rasmussen would eventually find her and win.

The nightmare he'd had the night before drifted through his mind. He had to protect her, even if it meant putting himself on the line to do it.

He didn't intend to kiss her, but one minute he was looking into her frightened eyes, the next, his mouth was on hers and all he could think about was how good she felt against him.

She melted in his arms. He marveled in the feel of her body against his. The softness of her curves. The sweet scent of her hair against his cheek. The heady taste of her mouth. The electrical current of arousal burning hot in his veins.

Blood pounded in his groin. They'd made love twice the night before, but already he was hard and wanting her again. His need for her was insane. With the feel of her body branded into his mind, he knew he would never get enough.

Backing her against the counter, he kissed her long and hard and deep. Her arms went around his shoulders. He loosened the knot of her robe and slipped his hands inside reveling in the warm softness of her skin. He brushed his fingertips against the hardened peaks of her nipples, and she shuddered in response.

In the back of his mind he heard a low humming, but he was too intent on kissing Leigh to pay much attention.

A hard knock at the door sent his hand to the pistol at the small of his back. He scrambled away, put his finger to his lips. "Go to the bedroom and wait for me," he whispered.

"Be careful," she whispered and slipped from the room.

Jake went to the door and checked the peephole. He swung open the door, his gaze skimming over Rick Monteith and landing on Mike Madrid.

"What the hell is he doing here?" he asked, referring to Madrid.

"He's going to stay here with Leigh while you and I nab Rasmussen." He sniffed. "You got coffee?"

Leave it to Monteith to tick him off even more than he'd been before opening the door. "What I got is a big problem with him." Jake punctuated the last word with a rude point at the dark haired man standing a few feet away.

Face dark with anger, Mike Madrid stepped forward. "You got something on your mind, Vanderpol, maybe you ought to lay it out."

Jake didn't hesitate. "As far as I know you gave up our location to Rasmussen."

"Son of a—" Madrid lunged at Jake.

Rick caught his arm and hauled him back before either man could throw a punch. "Knock it off." He jammed a finger at Jake. "Madrid didn't give you up any more than I did."

Muttering a profanity, Madrid shook off Rick's hands. "I'm out of here." Turning on his heel, he started for the SUV parked in the driveway with a brisk stride.

"Madrid!" Rick called out.

But Madrid didn't slow down. He didn't even look back.

"Damn it, Vanderpol."

"Screw him," Jake said.

"Bull." Rick poked a finger into his chest. "You have about two seconds to call him back."

"We don't need him."

"Madrid is going to keep an eye on your woman, my man. If you want to keep her safe, I suggest you get your head out of your ass and get him back here."

"How do I know he didn't give us up?" Jake asked.

"Because I trust him with my life," Rick said. "That's going to have to be good enough for you."

Jake cursed.

Rick sighed. "Maybe Cutter was right about you. Maybe when it comes to her you think with a different part of your anatomy than your brain."

"What part of his anatomy would that be?"

Both men swung around. Jake groaned

when he spotted Leigh standing in the hall. The look on her face told him she'd heard every word of the exchange.

"Leigh…"

"I want to know what's going on." She'd dressed in jeans, a turtleneck and a blue flannel shirt. Her face was pale and she was eyeing both of them with unconcealed hostility.

"We're here to help you get Rasmussen." Monteith looked at Jake and shook his head. "He's not cooperating."

She crossed to Jake. "You can't do this on your own. Let them help you."

The front door stood open. Beyond Jake heard a car door slam, and he cursed.

Leigh looked at Rick. "Who's out there?"

"Mike Madrid," Jake spat.

Her eyes widened. "The man who—"

"He didn't," Rick cut in. "I'll stake my life on that. He's here to help. Like me. Jake ticked him off."

"He's got a real knack for that," Leigh said dryly.

Rick grinned at Jake. "She knows you pretty well, eh?"

Jake scrubbed a hand over his face. The

truth of the matter was he trusted Rick Monteith with his life. If Rick said Madrid was on the level, Jake had no choice but to believe him.

Shoving his pride aside, he brushed past Rick and headed out the door. Madrid was kneeling at a trailer hitch upon which two snowmobiles were parked. He didn't look up when Jake approached.

"I trust Rick's judgment," Jake said. "If he says you're on the level, I believe him."

Madrid frowned. "You suck at apologies."

"Yeah, that's what everyone tells me."

He finished with the hitch, then rose to his full height. Jake took that moment to extend his hand. "Let's nab us a bad guy," he said, and the two men shook hands.

Chapter Sixteen

"So the story ran in this morning's edition?" Rick Monteith asked.

"And the online edition," Jake said.

"That Rasmussen could read from anywhere," Mike Madrid put in.

Leigh stood at the counter in the small kitchen and poured four cups of coffee. It didn't surprise her that her hands were shaking; her nerves were as tight as piano wires. As soon as they got the go-ahead from Ronald Waite telling them the call had been traced by Rasmussen, it was showtime.

She carried the tray to the table and sat down next to Jake. His gaze met hers. "You okay?" he asked.

No, she thought. She wasn't okay. Not by a long shot. She hated this plan. She hated putting Jake and the other two men in danger. She didn't want anyone getting hurt. But she knew if she wanted her life back— if she wanted Jake to have his life back—she was going to have to face this nightmare once and for all. "I'm okay," she said.

He squeezed her hand, then his gaze swept to each of the other two men. "This is how it's going to go down." He spread a small, computer-generated map on the table. "Leigh stays here with Madrid. Rick, as soon as we get the call from Ronald, we take the snowmobiles to the other cabin. It's exactly twelve miles from here." He set his finger on the map. "Across this frozen lake. There's a shed at the rear of the property. We stash the snowmobiles there and wait for Rasmussen to show."

"Rules of engagement?" Rick asked.

"Same as law enforcement. We use whatever force is necessary for us to safely bring him in, including deadly force."

Deadly force. God...

The phone on the counter beeped, and Jake got up and hit the speaker key. "Vanderpol."

"Rasmussen bit," came Ronald's voice on the other end. "We gave him the location of the cabin. Trace tells us he's in Toronto."

"No doubt he's got a private jet at his disposal. So we have to figure he can be in the area in just over an hour. We need to move." Jake released the call then turned to face them. "Time to rock and roll."

The next minutes passed in a blur. The men gathered weapons, and put on their coats and cold-weather gear. As Jake prepared to leave, it was as if she no longer existed. He was so focused on what he was about to he didn't even spare her a glance. It all boiled down to the job for him. Just like before; once he'd had Rasmussen in his sights, he hadn't so much as spared her a single thought.

Leigh knew it was petty of her to feel that way. Jake and the other two men were facing a dangerous enemy. They *needed* to be wholly focused on the coming hours. Maybe the reason she felt so bereft was because they had used her six years ago....

Struggling against the thoughts, she followed the men as far as the porch and watched Jake and Rick Monteith don their helmets.

Rick had already started his engine. Jake looked her way, then tossed the helmet into the snow and jogged toward the porch, his eyes dark and intent on her. She had a moment to brace. Then his arms wrapped around her. His mouth found hers. The kiss stirred her despite the circumstances.

"Don't be afraid," he whispered.

"I'm afraid for you."

He cupped her face in his large, strong hands. "We're going to be fine."

Her legs went weak when he kissed her again. Then he ran to the snowmobile. Leigh watched them disappear down the lane, praying he was right.

RONALD WAITE LIVED in an upscale suburb between Ann Arbor and Detroit, Michigan. He had a story buzzing around in his head and had decided to take the afternoon off and write it on his laptop computer at home. He let himself in through the front door of his two-story home and hung his coat in the closet. He was midway through the living room when he noticed that something didn't feel right about the house.

Uneasy, he listened, his mind scrolling through a quick security checklist. He glanced into the kitchen and saw the miniblinds at the back door stir. Then, feeling a chill in the air, he knew someone had broken into his house.

He backed toward the door, his hand going into his coat pocket for his cell phone. He turned and darted toward the door only to have his way blocked by two men who'd descended the stairs leading to the bedrooms. They were wearing black coats, ski masks, black leather gloves. *Killers,* he thought, and tried to lunge past them to get to the door. But the man nearest him slid a neat, chrome pistol from beneath his coat.

"Don't even think about it," the man said.

Ronald raised his hands, his eyes darting from man to man. "What do you want?"

"Information." The second man slid a shotgun from beneath his coat.

"Wh-what information?" Ronald asked.

"We want to know where Leigh Michaels is," the first man said.

He'd been in some tight situations in the years he'd worked at the *Investigator.* He'd certainly made some enemies. But he'd never felt as if his life were in danger. Looking at Rasmussen's men, he had a terrible feeling he wasn't going to survive this.

"I…I don't know where she is," he lied.

The men exchanged glances. The first man shook his head. "Look," he began, "we can do this easy or we can do it hard. Either way, you *will* tell us where she is."

Ronald's heart was beating so fast he thought he was going to have a heart attack.

"Turn around and give me your wrists," ordered one of the men, removing a pair of handcuffs from his coat pocket.

Ronald spun and threw himself into a run. He hit the dining room at full speed. His hand was in his pocket, seeking his cell phone. If he could just dial 911…

He heard a loud crack. Something stung him in the leg. Pain zinged through his body, and he fell facedown in the kitchen.

When he looked up, one of the men was standing over him, holding a stun gun in his hand. The man knelt, and Ronald felt himself being rolled onto his stomach. His hands were jerked roughly behind his back. The cuffs snapped into place.

Then the man rolled him onto his back. "You have ten seconds to tell us where she is."

Ronald knew if he told them where she was, Leigh Michaels was as good as dead. He didn't know what to do. Save himself and let Ian Rasmussen murder a young woman in cold blood? Or forfeit his own life so that she could live?

Perhaps he could lie to them, give them a false location, buy some time. Ideas spun through his mind. Surely he could think of something.

One of the men knelt next to Ronald. His eyes sought Ronald's. "Where is she?" he asked.

Ronald shook his head. "I don't know."

The man sighed, then brandished the stun gun. "This particular stun gun will put between one hundred thousand and five hundred thousand volts into your body. You just got a taste of what one hundred thousand volts feels like." He smiled. "Unpleasant, isn't it?"

"I don't know where she is," Ronald cried. "I swear!"

"Let's see what five hundred thousand

volts feels like." The man adjusted a knob on the gun.

Terror swept through Ronald when the man jammed the probes against his side. He cried out as five hundred thousand volts of electricity discharged into his body.

"Tell us and we won't have to hurt you any more," the man said.

"I...don't...know..."

Another loud crack sounded when the probes touched his skin. Writhing in agonizing pain, he knew he couldn't take much more.

"Tell us where she is and we'll let you go."

Sweating and panting like an animal, Ronald sobbed. "All right. Please! No more."

"Talk," the thug said.

Ronald Waite started to talk.

EVEN THOUGH THEY'D DONNED heavy weather gear, Jake was frozen to his bones when they arrived at the other cabin. At forty miles per hour, the windchill had hovered at a numbing thirty below zero. The trip across the lake had taken almost fifteen minutes.

He hadn't wanted to leave Leigh behind.

He knew how much could happen in fifteen minutes. But he also knew she was safer there than she would be here. He fully expected Rasmussen to show. When he did, the situation would undoubtedly turn ugly. He didn't want Leigh anywhere near it.

He and Rick stashed the snowmobiles in the shed behind the cabin. Even though it would be dark by the time Rasmussen showed up, Rick spent ten minutes covering the tracks. Jake went inside and built a fire in the hearth. He'd just finished when the door swung open and Rick walked inside.

"Why can't these situations ever happen when it's seventy degrees and sunny?" he grumbled.

Jake laughed. "Makes our job way too easy."

"Speaking of job…" Rick worked off his parka and gloves. "You need to call Cutter and give him a heads-up."

Jake knew he was right. Cutter needed to know about this. The man was going to be royally ticked off.

Not wanting to get chewed out in front of his fellow agent, Jake picked up his cell phone and took it to the bedroom. He removed his gloves and parka, then sat down on the bed and dialed the number.

Cutter answered on the first ring. "I was wondering when the hell you were going to check in."

"I'm checking in."

"I ought to fire you for insubordination, Vanderpol."

"Maybe you ought to wait until I hand you Rasmussen."

A beat of tense silence. *"What?"*

"I set up a sting—"

Cutter cursed harshly. "You set up a sting without my authorization!"

"I set up a sting because evidently you couldn't pull it off," Jake said evenly.

"If I were there I'd deck you."

"Don't worry, Cutter. You'll get your chance. I'll have him in custody by nineteen hundred."

"Jake, damn it, if anyone gets hurt."

"No one's going to get hurt."

"I want Rasmussen alive."

"I don't plan to kill him, but if it comes down to me or him, I'll take him out."

Another curse burned through the line. "Where are you and I'll send backup."

Jake was tempted to tell him. He and Rick needed all the help they could get. But Sean Cutter was a by-the-book superior. Jake wouldn't put it past him to call off the entire operation. With Leigh's life hanging in the balance, he couldn't risk that.

"I'll let you know when we have him in custody."

"Jake, damn it, you don't have the authority—"

Jake hit the end button and rose.

"...if anyone gets hurt..."

Cutter's words rang uncomfortably in his ears. It was Jake's biggest concern. Worry gnawed at him. He wanted to call Leigh to check on her. He desperately wanted to hear her voice. He missed her. Only half an hour had passed and already he was desperate to see her again.

The next thought that struck him threatened to buckle his legs, and he sat down hard on the bed. Was it possible he'd never stopped loving her?

The thought terrified him because no matter how carefully he'd laid out this plan there was always the chance something could go wrong. But the thought of loving her again—of her returning that love thrilled him in equal measure.

Jake had taken lovers in the six years since he'd been with her. He'd enjoyed being with them, even cared for them. But none of the women he'd known had even come close to touching him the way Leigh did.

He found Rick sitting at the kitchen table, sipping instant coffee. The other man grinned when Jake approached. "Cutter rake you over the coals?"

Jake made a sound of disgust, then went to the sink and snagged a cup even though he despised instant. "Let's go over the plan again," he said.

"We've already been over it three ti—"

"We go over it again!" Jake snapped.

Rick sighed. "Whatever you say, partner."

Jake carried his coffee to the table and sat down. His hand shook when he raised the cup to his lips.

"You got it bad for her, huh, Jake?"

Jake stared into his coffee. "If anything

happens to her, I swear I'll kill him with my bare hands."

Rick looked at him as if seeing him for the first time. "I'll be damned, Iron Jake, I don't think I've ever seen you like this."

Jake muttered a curse.

"Nothing's going to happen to her. This is a clean plan. He thinks she's here. He'll come. He gets us instead." Grinning, Rick patted the weapon strapped to his side. "He'll have some firepower, but so do we. Everyone goes home except Rasmussen."

Jake only hoped there wasn't some loose end they hadn't thought of.

LEIGH STOOD AT THE WINDOW watching dusk descend. An hour had passed since Jake and Rick had left, but it felt like a lifetime. She tried not to worry, but the thought of Jake facing off with Rasmussen made her realize just how much she'd come to care for him.

As hard as she'd tried not to, she'd fallen for Jake all over again. Fallen for him even harder than she had six years ago. Was he going to walk away and leave her life in tatters again? Was the job always going to come first? Once he got Rasmussen, would he still need her?

She knew in her heart that Jake was a good man. She knew he had the most honorable of intentions. But he was a warrior. Even though he was currently at odds with the MIDNIGHT Agency, Leigh knew Sean Cutter wouldn't let him go. Jake was too good at what he did. She knew Jake would go back if asked. The question foremost in her mind was, where did that leave her?

She jumped when she heard movement behind her.

Mike Madrid smiled and shoved a mug of something hot and steaming at her. "It's getting colder. I thought you might like some hot chocolate," he said.

Leigh reached for the mug. "Thank you."

He looked uncomfortable for a moment, cleared his throat. "I just want you to know I didn't give up your location. Rasmussen is a techno freak. Likes to surround himself with a lot of high-tech equipment."

She'd already figured that out. "Jake would never have left if he believed you had given us up."

Madrid nodded. For the first time, Leigh noticed the rifle at his side. She caught a glimpse of a shoulder holster beneath his parka. "I scoped out the cabin and the property. The best place for me is on the roof."

"It's ten degrees out there," Leigh said.

"I'm dressed for it. That's where I'll have the best view. I can see anything coming from all directions. I can use the chimney for cover." He knocked on the Kevlar vest at his chest. "I'm pretty well protected."

"Is there anything I should be doing?" she asked.

"Just stay aware. Be cautious. Don't let anyone in." He slid a tiny pistol from his jeans and passed it to her. "I don't expect any problems, but if something does arise, I want you to shoot first and ask questions later."

Her heart was beating hard and fast when she looked down at the piece of deadly steel in her hands.

"Keep it near you at all times. This should be over in the next couple of hours, but he could keep us waiting."

He started to turn away, but Leigh reached out and touched his shoulder. He turned dark, surprised eyes on her. "Thank you," she said.

"Thank me when this is over," he said, and walked out the door.

Chapter Seventeen

Leigh paced the cabin like a trapped animal. She hadn't heard from Mike Madrid since he'd gone up to the roof twenty minutes ago. She wanted to call Jake, but didn't want to distract him during a potentially crucial moment. If anything happened, she assured herself, he would call her. She hadn't let her cell phone out of her sight since he'd left.

She put another log on the fire even though it was already blazing. In the kitchen she made tea, but she didn't want it. She couldn't sit still, couldn't stop pacing. She couldn't stop thinking about Jake and all the things that could go wrong.

"Please be careful," she whispered as she walked to the window and spread the curtains.

At some point the wind had picked up. Leigh could hear it howling around the cabin. Usually she didn't mind being alone, but tonight she felt as if she were the only human being in the world. A world that was suddenly hostile and dangerous. It was going to be a very long night.

She was about to drop the curtain and warm herself at the fire when movement at the edge of the woods snagged her attention. With the snow and darkness she couldn't be sure, but she thought she'd seen something move. Had it been a deer moving within the trees? Were the fear and her own nerves playing tricks on her? Or had she seen something that warranted her alerting Mike Madrid?

He'd told her he was equipped with night-vision equipment. Surely he would notice if someone approached the cabin. She was probably jumping at shadows. The result of high stress and an active imagination.

But in the six years Leigh had been on the run, she'd learned to trust her instincts. Right now those instincts were telling her to err on the side of caution and find Mike Madrid.

Setting the tea on the mantel above the hearth, she slipped into her coat. At the foyer she stepped into her boots, then went out the door. The cold was brittle and took her breath. The night was so quiet, she could hear the tinkle of snow striking the ground. Following Mike's footsteps, she silently made her way to the rear of the cabin. He'd used the picnic table and stone chimney to climb to the roof.

"Mike?"

She waited a full minute, but he didn't respond. She didn't want to make any noise, but thought he should know she'd seen something in the woods.

"Mike? Are you there? Can you hear me?"

When he didn't answer she trudged through snow to the side of the cabin. "Mike?"

Struggling to stay calm, Leigh went back around the rear of the cabin. "Madrid?" she said more loudly.

Growing increasingly uneasy, she started toward the front of the cabin. Since she couldn't get him to answer, she would call him on his cell. He'd changed it to vibration, so the ringing would not make any noise in case there was someone nearby.

She was midway to the door when she spotted something dark in the snow. At first she thought someone had dumped coffee. Kneeling, she set her hand against the dark stain. Her heart slammed against her ribs when the metallic stench of blood filled her nostrils.

Stumbling to her feet, Leigh hurled herself into a dead run. She tore around the corner of the cabin at a dangerous speed and burst through the front door. Everything appeared as she had left it. Fire crackling in the hearth. Mug of tea on the mantel. Cell phone on the coffee table.

But she realized the pistol she'd left next to the phone was gone. Then suddenly she noticed the melting snow on the floor. Someone was in the cabin. "Mike?" she called out.

Sensing danger, she darted toward the cell phone. She was midway there when she saw two men coming out of the kitchen, one carrying a rifle, the other a pistol.

She spun to run to the door, and found herself face-to-face with Ian Rasmussen. Tall and elegant in a long leather coat, black gloves and a cashmere scarf, he stood just two feet away from her, watching her with cold, dispassionate eyes.

Leigh had always believed she'd faced her worst nightmare six years ago. Only now did she realized she'd been wrong. Facing Ian Rasmussen now, knowing he would show her no mercy when he dealt with her—when he dealt with Jake—was her worst nightmare.

A nightmare that was just beginning.

JAKE HAD TAKEN UP a position on the roof of the cabin. Rick Monteith waited inside. They'd only been at the cabin an hour, but it seemed like forever. He was worried as hell about Leigh. He knew there was no way Rasmussen could find her, but he couldn't quiet the little voice inside his head telling him she was in danger.

Shifting position in the snow, he put his eye to the scope and adjusted the sight. The scope was perfectly adjusted. The plan was well laid. They were going to get through this, he assured himself. Once Rasmussen was behind bars, Jake was going to spend some time getting reacquainted with Leigh. He wanted to make up for lost time. Earn her trust again. Love her the way she deserved to be loved…

The cell phone clipped to his belt vibrated. He snatched it up, checked the window and was startled to see Mike Madrid's name. "Why the hell are you calling me?" he snapped.

"Rasmussen…"

Jake knew immediately something was wrong. He barely recognized Mike's voice, it was that weak. He sat up, gripped the phone tightly. "What happened?"

"Bastard…has Leigh."

Terror turned Jake's blood to ice. "Where?"

"Here…cabin…"

"Jesus, Madrid. Are you hit?"

"Went right through…the vest. Hurry…"

But Jake was already scrambling off the roof, taking the stepladder to the rear porch. "I'm on my way," he said.

But the phone had gone dead.

He burst through the rear door. Rick Monteith raised his rifle in the instant before he saw it was Jake. "For crying out loud, Vanderpol, I just about plugged—"

"Madrid is down. Rasmussen is at the cabin." He nearly choked on the words as another layer of terror closed around his throat like a fist. "He has Leigh."

Monteith was already grabbing his outdoor gear, cursing, his face taut. "How bad is Madrid hurt?"

"He sounded bad." Jake's phone vibrated. *Madrid*, he thought, and snatched it up. "Yeah."

"Ah, Mr. Vanderpol."

Rage and terror and a hundred other impotent emotions tore through him at the sound of Rasmussen's voice. "You lay a hand on her and I'll kill you with my bare hands," he ground out.

Rasmussen laughed. "Maybe I've already laid a hand on her. Maybe while you were playing secret agent, I was making up for six years of lost time."

Jake's heart beat madly in his chest, pumping fury to every cell in his body. He could hear himself breathing hard. He was conscious of Rick touching his arm, speaking to him, but he was so focused on Rasmussen he couldn't comprehend the words.

"What do you want?" he managed after a moment.

"I want you to come to me, of course. I believe we have a score to settle."

"Let me speak to Leigh."

Static sounded, then Leigh's voice filled the line. "Don't do it, Jake! He'll kill you!"

"Are you all right?" he asked. "Did he hurt you?"

But it was Rasmussen's voice that answered. "You have ten minutes to get here. I want you alone and unarmed. If I so much as mistake a deer for another agent, I will slit her throat. Do you understand?"

"I understand," Jake said.

"Ten minutes, Mr. Vanderpol. If you don't show, I will kill her, and you'll be left to put all the pieces of her back together."

"Don't hurt her, damn it," Jake snapped. "I'll be there."

"If you're not here in—" he paused "—nine minutes, her blood will be on your hands."

The phone went dead. Jake had already calculated how long it would take him to get across the lake. He'd have to push it to be there in nine minutes. "I have to go," he heard himself say.

"Don't you dare run off half-cocked, Vanderpol." Rick followed him to the rear door.

When Jake didn't stop, Rick reached out and grasped his shoulder, turned him around. "You can't go alone."

"If I don't get there in nine minutes, that son of a bitch is going to kill her."

"You know the rules, Vanderpol. No agent ever goes in without backup."

Snarling an expletive, Jake tried to shake off the other man's grip. "There's no time for a plan."

Rick maintained his grip. "I'll improvise."

Jake knew the other man was right. But it was his heart driving him now, not logic. The mere thought of Leigh with Rasmussen was enough to send him into a panic. He couldn't bear the thought of her being hurt.

Lifting the rifle strap over his shoulder, he set the weapon on the kitchen table. He removed his pistol holster, but slid the Glock into the waistband of his jeans. He knew enough about Rasmussen to know he was a liar. There was no way he was going to show up unarmed. He knew when he arrived Rasmussen would not only kill him, but he would kill Leigh, as well. Jake wasn't going to let that happen.

Or die trying.

"Vanderpol, don't go off the deep end, man. Come on. Stay with me."

"If Rasmussen sees you, he'll kill her," he ground out.

"Then I'll just have to make sure he doesn't see me."

"How are you going to manage that? The snowmobiles aren't exactly quiet. We have to assume he has Madrid's night-vision goggles. He'll spot you a mile away."

"I'll ditch the snowmobile when I get within earshot. Cover the rest of the distance on foot."

It was as good a plan as they were going to come up with in thirty seconds. "Do it." Jake started for the door. "Madrid was wearing a vest. Be advised that bastard has armor-piercing bullets. I've got to go."

He sprinted to the shed and started the snowmobile. "I'll try to draw Rasmussen out," Jake said. "If I can't get him outside, I'll try to get him near a window."

"If I can get off a shot, I'll take him out," Rick said.

Jake gassed the snowmobile. Rick jumped aside as Jake shot through the door. Then it was just him and Rasmussen and a life-or-death race against time.

LEIGH KNEW all too well what would happen if Jake showed, so she lunged for the phone. But one of the men grabbed her from behind, yanking her back.

"Don't do it!" she yelled, hoping Jake could hear her. "He'll kill you!"

But Rasmussen had already hit the end button. His expression was coldly amused when he turned to Leigh. "Loverboy is on his way, my love. I gave him ten minutes. Do you think he can make it?"

"I think you're insane," she said in a shaking voice.

Rasmussen looked at the man holding her. "Release her."

Leigh scrambled away. "Where's Mike Madrid?" she asked.

"Let's just say a hollow-point bullet will penetrate even the most high-tech body armor."

Remembering the blood, Leigh choked back a sob. She couldn't believe this man whom she'd once known intimately could be so cold-blooded. How could she have been so wrong about him?

"What do you want with me?" she asked.

"I think that's obvious." His gaze raked over her. "You and I have some unfinished business, don't you think?"

"What I think," she said, "is that you are a sick son of a bitch."

Rasmussen smiled. "I'm going to enjoy breaking you down, Kelsey. We've so much to…discuss."

"I have nothing to say to you."

He stepped closer. "But I have so very much to say to you."

She took a step back. "For God's sake, Ian, you have a chance to flee the country. Why don't you just go?"

"Because I've waited six years for this moment. Some days, sitting in my cell, the only thing that kept me going was the thought of putting my hands on you. Of killing Vanderpol. I'm going to make this memorable for both of us."

His words, the way he was looking at her, made her feel more frightened than she'd ever been in her life. "Don't." Glancing over her shoulder, she took in the sight of the two other men in the room. Both were armed, and she knew if she tried to run they would put a bullet in her back.

"Besides, I could hardly leave the country without saying goodbye to you, could I?" he said. "I've missed you."

"You missed your freedom, not me."

He continued as if he hadn't heard her. "Do you have any idea what six years in a cage does to a man?"

"Please don't hurt anyone else, Ian." Her voice quavered, but she couldn't help it. "You have the money to go anywhere in the world. Leave the country while you still can."

"My entire *life* revolved around you!" he shouted abruptly. "I gave you everything. *Everything!* The penthouse. The Jaguar. My heart."

"You don't have a heart." The words were out before she could stop them.

Something dark and frightening flashed in the depths of his eyes. *Rage,* she thought, and shivered.

"I'd even bought a diamond ring for you," he said. "A lovely marquis-cut yellow stone from South Africa. It was one of a kind. Six carats. Flawless. I never got the chance to give it you."

Leigh hadn't known about the ring, but it didn't matter. Whatever had happened between them six years ago was a mistake. A terrible mistake made by the starstruck twenty-one-year-old she'd been.

"I gave you everything," he said. "*Everything.* And how do you repay me?"

Leigh took another step back. There were three ways out of the cabin. Through the front door. Through the living room window. Or through the door in the kitchen at the rear of the cabin. The urge to run was strong, but she knew there was no escape.

"You repay me by sleeping with the very man who would ultimately destroy my life."

"You destroyed your own life."

"How do you think that made me feel, Kelsey? I trusted you. You betrayed me."

"You sold weapons to terrorists. Surely you had to know there would be repercussions."

"I'm a businessman in a world economy. An economy where it's all about supply and demand."

Unable to control her anger, she blurted out, "What are you going to do, Ian? Shoot me in the back? Is that why you're here? Is that somehow going to make everything all right?"

His smile chilled her. "You still have a temper, don't you, my love? I always loved to see you angry."

"The only thing you love is yourself."

He crossed to her in two strides. His hand shot out so quickly, she didn't have time to duck. The blow snapped her head back, sent her reeling. "You would be wise to keep your smart mouth in check," he said.

Leigh shook off the dizziness and pain. She felt the sting of a cut on her lip and tasted blood. Tears burned her eyes, but she didn't let them fall. She would not give him the satisfaction of seeing her cry.

"Go to hell," she choked.

Without warning, his hand snaked out. His fingers clamped down on her arm like a vise. The next thing she knew she was being dragged toward the rear bedroom. Leigh fought him with every ounce of strength she possessed. She dug in her heels, clawed at the doorway as they passed through it. But her strength was no match for his.

Once in the bedroom, he kicked the door shut behind them and shoved her onto the bed. Before she could scramble off, he was on top of her, using his weight to push her back.

"Get off me!" she yelled.

She tried to twist away, but he was too heavy. She nearly gagged when his mouth descended. She turned her head, but he forced his mouth to hers. She struggled with all the strength she had to get free of him.

Then, surprising her, he rolled off her and rose. Leigh sprang from the bed, and they faced each other, the only sound their labored breathing.

"It's too bad Vanderpol didn't send you back here to sleep with me again."

Despite the circumstances, the words hurt. "He would never do that," she said.

"Ah, but he did the last time, didn't he? His kind of love is...flexible, no?"

She hated that this man had the power to hurt her.

"I would have appreciated bedding you one more time. Unfortunately, we're nearly out of time." He looked at his watch. "Your lover has four minutes left."

"He won't come." But she knew Jake would come for her.

"Yes, he will." Never taking his eyes from hers, Rasmussen pushed open the door. "Donovan."

One of the men appeared in the hall. Leigh watched as a silent communication passed between them, then Donovan removed handcuffs from the pocket of his coat.

"Put them on her." Rasmussen snapped his fingers and the second man appeared. "Vanderpol will be here in about three minutes. I want you to go out to the lake. Take the chain saw. Cut a hole in the ice." His gaze flicked to Leigh. "Make it large enough for a human body to pass through. Take the rifle with you. I'll meet you there."

"Yes, sir." The man hustled away.

The first man limped toward her, cuffs in hand. When she saw his pale eyes, his pockmarked and angular face and long black hair pulled into a ponytail, she recognized him as the man who'd accosted her in the motel the day she'd left Denver. The man she'd stabbed in the calf.

"I'm going to enjoy seeing you die," he said quietly.

Terrified, she shoved past Rasmussen and ran toward the door.

"Stop her!" Rasmussen shouted.

Somehow she made it through the door. Ran blindly down the hall. Into the living room. She heard footsteps and shouting behind her as she careered toward the front door. Arms outstretched she hit the door, slammed her hand against the lock.

Then a pair of strong arms grabbed hold of her. She lashed out with her feet as he swung her around. The next thing she knew she was being flung to the floor. She fought madly, but the man overpowered her, rolling her onto her stomach. She felt her hands being jerked behind her, the cuffs clicking into place.

Jake, she thought, and her screams turned to sobs.

Chapter Eighteen

The snowmobile roared over the snow at a death-defying speed. Trees blurred by. Jake hadn't bothered with a helmet, and the wind and snow were stinging his eyes. But the physical discomforts were nothing compared to the horrors inside his head.

Rasmussen had Leigh. He was depraved. Had been in prison for six years. And he was capable of extreme violence.

The lights of the cabin loomed into view. He smelled wood smoke from the fire in the hearth. Though the visibility was poor because of the falling snow, he was still able to make out three snowmobiles parked half a mile from the driveway. He drew closer to the cabin. He was within rifle range now. He could feel the eyes watching him through the crosshairs.

He parked the snowmobile fifty yards from the cabin and killed the engine. A stark and eerie silence filled his ears. Raising his hands to shoulder level, he started toward the cabin. He watched for movement, any sign of life, but saw nothing.

Twenty yards from the front door he stopped, the pistol he'd tucked into his waistband pressing reassuringly against his back. "Rasmussen!" he shouted. "I'm here! Come get me!"

No answer.

Jake's heart began to hammer.

The cabin was deserted, he realized, and broke into a run toward the front door. Five yards out he spotted blood in the snow, and he went wild. All he could think was that they'd hurt Leigh. He dashed to the front door and burst into the cabin.

"Leigh!" he yelled. *"Leigh!"*

The only answer was the whistle of wind through the trees. The tinkle of snow against the windows. And the thrum of his own terror.

THE SNOWFALL WAS SO HEAVY Leigh couldn't see more than a few yards ahead. Rasmussen gripped her right arm. The thug with the limp walked beside her to her left. Twice she'd broken free and tried to run. Twice, hindered by the handcuffs, she'd been caught before getting more than a few yards.

They were on the lake and had been walking for ten minutes. All around the lake stretched like a vast frozen plain of endless white.

"Why are you doing this?" she asked Rasmussen. "Why didn't you just flee while you could?"

He stopped and gave her his full attention. "Because I have a reputation to maintain."

"Reputation?"

"You made a laughingstock of me, my love. You committed the ultimate sin when you betrayed me. No one betrays Ian Rasmussen and lives to tell about it. Especially a woman."

She cringed when he raised his hand and brushed the backs of his fingers over her cheek. "Don't think for a minute this is easy for me," he said. "I loved you."

This man had absolutely no idea what love was.

He leaned close to kiss her, but Leigh turned her head. "Don't," she said.

Rasmussen stepped back, his expression as cold and hard as the ice beneath her feet. "In a few minutes, my darling, you'll be begging me to forgive you."

Movement a few yards ahead drew her attention. For an instant she thought Jake had arrived to save her from what would surely be a terrible death. Her faint hope died, though, when they reached their destination.

The man in the parka had used a chain saw to cut a rectangular square the size of a bathtub in the ice. Next to the hole, a length of heavy chain was piled on the ice like a giant steel snake. It didn't take much imagination for her to realize what they were going to do to her.

Several yards away a small helicopter looked out of place on the ice. The pilot stood just outside its doors, smoking a cigarette.

"Any sign of Vanderpol?" Rasmussen asked.

The thug standing next to the hole in the ice shook his head. "Not yet."

"He's probably at the cabin," the man gripping her arm said.

Rasmussen looked toward the chopper. "I'd hoped he would be here to witness her death."

All three men glanced over at the pilot, who'd approached the group. "We need to take off now, Mr. Rasmussen. We've got lake-effect snow moving in. Visibility is dwindling fast. If the weather gets any worse, we could find ourselves stranded."

Rasmussen nodded, then his gaze landed on Leigh. "Put the chain on her."

Leigh had thought she knew the meaning of terror. But the thought of what they were going to do to her was worse than anything she could have imagined even in her nightmares. Her entire body began to tremble violently. Her heart beat out of control in her chest.

Rasmussen seemed to be enjoying her fear. "That twenty foot length of chain weighs almost a hundred pounds, my love. Once we wrap it around you and throw you into the water, you'll go down like a rock."

"Don't do this," she heard herself say.

"The water here is about forty feet deep,"

he told her. "The ice this far north doesn't melt completely until April. By then you'll be little more than bones. No one will ever find your body."

"You bastard," she choked.

One side of his mouth curved. "Goodbye, my darling." He nodded at the two men. "Do it."

The man in the ponytail bent to pick up one end of the heavy chain. The other man started toward her. Running would be futile. The odds of her getting away were slim to none. But her will to live would not let her go down without a fight.

She threw herself into a sprint. The handcuffs hampered her, but she didn't let them slow her down. She heard shouting behind her, but she didn't take time to look over her shoulder. She ran at a dangerous speed, plowing through snowdrifts, slipping on patches of ice, maintaining her balance by the sheer force of her will. "Jake!" she shouted. *"Jake! Help me!"*

In her peripheral vision she saw one of the men sprinting toward her off to her right. He was so close she could hear the crunching of his boots on the snow. Leigh veered left. She ran as fast as her legs would allow, sliding and stumbling.

Her leg muscles screamed with fatigue. Her heart threatened to burst. She didn't know how much ground she'd covered. It felt like miles. Then, seemingly out of nowhere a strong hand seized hold of her shoulder and spun her around. She caught a glimpse of a pock-marked face. Her legs tangled. She hit the ice hard, the breath rushing from her lungs.

The next thing she knew she was being jerked roughly to her feet. "Walk," the thug with the ponytail snapped.

Oh, dear God, this is it, she thought. *They're going to kill me.*

She had to face the terrifying reality that she wasn't going to get out of this. That she would never see Jake again. That she would never have the chance to tell him she loved him.

Her heart broke as she began the long walk to her death.

JAKE CLEARED THE CABIN in less than a minute. The whole time, terror clawed at him with the fervor of a frantic animal.

Where the hell had they taken Leigh? Was it her blood he'd seen in the snow? What had they done to her?

The thought of her injured and in pain tore him up inside. Struggling to remain calm, he stood in the living room. He had to focus if he was going to think this through. If he was going to find her in time to save her life.

"Easy, buddy," he muttered. "Come on. Think."

He looked around the living room. There were no weapons, which meant they'd taken whatever they'd had with them. He quickly searched the bedroom and kitchen but found nothing. He found a snow camouflage parka, pants and gloves in the mudroom. He went out the back door. That was when he remembered the three snowmobiles.

Rasmussen, his thugs and Leigh hadn't left the area. They'd merely left the cabin. But why had he taken her into the woods instead of making a run for it and taking her with him? What could he possibly have in mind?

Jake scanned the surrounding woods. Any

tracks they might have made had been covered by the falling snow. Then he remembered that the cabin wasn't far from the lake. Rasmussen might have taken her there. There were no trees, which would make an excellent landing point for a small chopper. Even though the lake was frozen with a foot of ice, a chainsaw would make short work of the ice. The deep water would be the perfect place to hide two bodies….

Dashing back inside, Jake tore off his snowmobile suit and stepped into the snow camouflage parka and pants. If the heavy snowfall continued, he might just be able to reach her before it was too late.

He sprinted through the woods, muscling through drifts and fallen logs. Branches scratched at his face and snagged his clothes, but he didn't slow down. His heart dropped when he spotted a person lying against a tree a dozen yards away. He looked down and saw blood in the snow. Plenty of it. *Leigh*, he thought, and sprinted to the tree.

Mike Madrid lay on his side, the snow surrounding him dark with blood. For a moment Jake thought he was dead. "Aw, man, no."

Then Madrid raised his head and cursed. "Took you long enough," he said weakly.

Jake began to assess the other man's injuries. "Easy, partner. Let me have a look at you."

Gently he rolled Madrid onto his back. The other man groaned. He'd been shot in the abdomen and was slowly bleeding out.

"Bastard has armor-piercing bullets," Madrid said.

Jake snatched up his cell phone and dialed Sean Cutter. Cutter picked up on the first ring.

"I got a man down," Jake said without preamble.

Cutter swore. "Who?"

"Madrid."

"How bad?"

"Code red."

"Where are you?"

"Michigan. Southeast of Sault Sainte Marie. I'll turn on his GPS. We got heavy weather, Sean."

"Anything else I need to know?"

"Come armed." Jake disconnected and turned to Madrid. "Where did they take Leigh?"

"I was in and out of consciousness for a while. But from what I gathered, they're going to kill her, drop her body through the ice," Madrid said, gasping for breath.

Jake broke a sweat beneath his winter gear.

As if the words had taken too much energy, Madrid closed his eyes. Jake reached out and touched the other man's shoulder. "You're going to be all right, partner."

"Go get that...son of a bitch."

Jake knew how painful a gut shot was and wished there was something he could do. He reached into Madrid's coat and pulled out his cell phone. Removing the back, he turned on the GPS chip all MIDNIGHT agents were required to have installed and tucked the phone back into Madrid's coat pocket. "Cutter's on the way with a medivac."

"Go get her, Vanderpol."

Jake squeezed Madrid's shoulder, then rose and started toward the lake. He ran for what seemed like miles. Abruptly the trees opened to a vast white plain Jake recognized as the lake. He skidded down the embankment and hit the ice running. Visibility was only a few yards. He had no idea which direction he was going. He didn't even know if his hunch was right. All he knew was that he was out of options.

He'd just hit his stride when a scream shattered the silence. He halted, listening.

"Jake! *Jaaaaake!* Help me!"

The terror in Leigh's voice shattered his heart. If he didn't get to her soon, it would be too late.

Adrenaline pumping full force through his body, Jake started in the direction of her screams.

LEIGH COULD FEEL the cold numbing her body as she trudged through the snow toward certain death. But even though she was terrified of the horrors that waited for her beneath the ice, she could only think of Jake. Oh, how she'd wanted to spend the rest of her life with him. That she would never get the chance broke her heart.

She shouted his name, but her voice was getting weak. The cold and terror working in tandem were zapping her strength. She'd sworn she wouldn't give Rasmussen the satisfaction of seeing her cry. But as the thug forced her closer to the hole in the ice, she had to choke back sobs.

The thug who'd caught her and was now taking her to Rasmussen had grown silent. Even his grip on her arm had loosened some. Leigh suspected he might have a smidgen of humanity left in the shell of his heart, but she knew it was not enough to save her. She knew Rasmussen would kill anyone who got in the way of his goal, including his own men.

She stumbled on the ice where the surface had buckled, and fell to her knees, sobbing openly now. Wherever Jake was, she prayed he was safe.

"Get up, lady."

The thug's voice reached her as if from a great distance. Not certain she had the strength to rise, she looked up. The snow was coming down so hard she could barely make out his expression.

"I need to rest," she said.

"You're going to get plenty of rest where you're going." He took her arm. "Let's go."

A shift in light behind him caught her attention. A spec of gray.

"All right," she said. But she didn't move, looking at the speck of gray she'd seen earlier. It was moving closer. At first she thought it was a bear or deer perhaps. Then she realized it was a man dressed in full snow camouflage gear running toward them.

One of the agents from MIDNIGHT? Had Jake come through for her after all? Suddenly it dawned on her that if the thug straightened and looked behind him, whomever was approaching would be dead in a fraction of a second. She needed to distract her captor.

"I...I think I sprained my ankle," she blurted.

The man glared at her. "Do I look like I care? Get up and walk or I'm going to drag you."

Leigh feigned difficulty rising. The thought of rescue made her almost giddy with hope. But the situation could still explode into violence any moment.

When the thug grasped her hair, she cried out in pain. "I said get up!"

She stumbled to her feet, the man's fingers digging into her arm, forcing her to walk.

"I think I'm going to faint," she said.

But her words were too late. He'd looked over his shoulder, squinting through the heavy snowfall. He spotted the person approaching, and froze.

He dropped to one knee, brought up the rifle and took aim. Leigh did the only thing she could, and rammed him with her shoulder. A gunshot shattered the silence.

"Bitch!" he snarled, butting her with the rifle and sending her flying backward into the snow.

As if in slow motion she saw the man bring up the rifle, set the scope to his eye and take aim at the figure in the distance.

"No!" she yelled, getting to her feet.

A gunshot rent the air, and the thug clutched his chest, his mouth opening and closing soundlessly. The rifle fell to the ground. Blood leaked between his fingers. Then he was falling forward...

Not sure who the figure in the distance was, Leigh began to run blindly through the snow, sobbing and choking. Then a hand slapped over her mouth, and the next thing she knew she was being tackled to the ground. She braced for the impact, but at the last minute her attacker twisted and she landed on top of him.

"Easy, honey. It's Jake. You're safe."

Relief rushed through her with such force that she couldn't speak. She couldn't think. All she could do was feel his body, solid and sure against her. Then she remembered that Rasmussen and at least two other men were waiting for them. That they planned to kill her. And if she and Jake wanted to live, they were going to have to act quickly.

Chapter Nineteen

Jake had never considered himself an emotional man. But even after ascertaining that Leigh was unhurt, he couldn't stop touching her.

She was trying to speak, but he kissed her. Not a sexual kiss, but a kiss that spoke of something much deeper, much more profound.

"We have to stop Rasmussen," she panted.

"I need to get you to safety," he said. "That's all that matters."

Taking her arm, he guided her back to where the thug had fallen. He went through the man's pockets. When he found the handcuff key, he turned her around and unlocked one of the cuffs.

After he did, she flung her arms around

him, and for several emotional minutes he did nothing but hold her and stroke her and whisper her name.

"He didn't hurt you?" Jake asked.

"No." She bit her lip. "What about Madrid?"

Jake grimaced. "He's down. Medivac's on the way." *If the weather holds,* he thought.

"Let's go." Careful to be gentle with her, he guided her in the general direction of the cabin, but she dug in her heels and stopped.

"No." Shaking off his grip, Leigh stopped and turned to face him. "We can't let him get away."

"I don't care about Rasmussen," Jake said. "All I care about is you." He only wished he'd said those words six years ago.

She blinked back tears. "Jake, we have to stop him. We can't let him get away with what he's done."

"I'm not going to risk your getting hurt."

"I'm your only hope of stopping him." She pointed at the swirling white expanse of the lake. "He's out there, waiting for his thug to .eturn with me. There'ᶜ a chopper waiting. He's going to kill me and flee the country."

"No," he said.

She got in his face. "Jake, we have to do this."

"I did it six years ago and I've regretted it ever since!"

"You did the right thing!" she shouted back.

Jake couldn't believe what he was hearing. Couldn't believe what he was *feeling*. He'd never forgiven himself for not stopping her six years ago. Now she wanted to do the same thing all over again. Only, this time she knew fully that Rasmussen planned to kill her.

"If we don't do this, we may as well hand our futures to Rasmussen. Let me tell you something, Jake. I'm not going to do it. I'm sick of having to move every six months. Never living in any one place long enough to make friends."

"We have each other." But he knew it was a weak rationalization.

"He'll go after your family," she said. "Your fellow agents."

Jake thought of Madrid and a wave of fresh fury washed through him. He hated it, but she was right. "Okay," he ground out. "But we do it on my terms."

JAKE DONNED the thug's trench coat and ski mask. Tucking his pistol into his pocket, he picked up the thug's rifle. He loosely secured the cuffs at Leigh's wrists. He hated seeing her hands bound, but if they were going to pull this off, they had to make it look believable.

He found a second pistol in the thug's boot and dropped it into Leigh's coat pocket. "If anything happens, you can tug on the cuffs. The left one is loose. The right one is locked in place."

When she nodded, he was suddenly overcome by doubt and wanted to nix the entire idea. The plan was incredibly dangerous. Too dangerous. He couldn't bear the thought of her getting hurt. "I want you to shoot first and ask questions later. You got that?"

Even frightened and disheveled, she was breathtakingly beautiful. But her eyes were dark with fear. Fear he wished she'd never had to feel.

"I can handle it."

He didn't think she could. Hell, *he* could barely handle this and he was a trained agent. "You're way over your head, Leigh."

"So are you."

He wasn't sure if she was talking about the crazy plan they were going to try to pull off or his feelings for her. He figured she was right on both counts.

Jake looked around and wondered where Rick Monteith was. Even the most experienced outdoorsman could find himself in trouble when the snow was coming down this hard. Add a madman with a rifle and armor-piercing bullets to the mix and it was possible Monteith might never find his way to them.

Tugging his cell from his pocket, he hit Monteith's speed dial. The other man picked up on the first ring.

"Where the hell are you?" Monteith asked.

"On the lake. You?"

"I picked up Madrid's SOS. I'm with him. Chopper's delayed because of this frickin' snow."

"How is he?"

A beat of silence. "Not good," Rick said in a low voice. "He doesn't have much time."

All MIDNIGHT agents were trained emergency medical technicians. But an EMT could only do so much in the field. Madrid needed a doctor. He needed fluids, maybe even a blood transfusion. Later he would probably need surgery to remove the bullet.

"Stay with him. I'm going after Rasmussen."

"Damn it, Jake. A team is on the way. Leave it to them."

"He's got a chopper on the lake ready to whisk him off. We wait and he's going to be gone."

"He would be crazy to fly in this weather."

Neither man spoke for a moment. Jake figured they both knew Rasmussen was as insane as they came. "Call me if you hear from Cutter," he said.

"Be careful, partner."

"Goes without saying," Jake said, and disconnected.

Leigh was standing just a foot away, her expression taut with concern. "How is Madrid?"

He considered sugarcoating it, but decided she deserved the truth. "He's in a bad way."

She put her hand over her mouth. "Is he going to make it?"

"I don't know, Leigh. All I can say is that he's young and strong. Rick's an EMT, and Cutter's doing his best to get a team here." He looked up at the falling snow, knowing Sean Cutter wouldn't let something like the weather keep him from a downed agent.

"We need to move," he said. "Here's how it's going to go down. Rasmussen and the other two men will believe I'm their third man. The ski mask will keep anyone from recognizing me. I'm going to act as if I'm bringing you back, but I'll put you down on the ice a good distance away. First chance I get, I take out either Rasmussen or the thug. If the pilot tries to bolt, I take him out, too. The key is stealth, Leigh. I need to get close to them without them realizing who I am. That will give me the upper hand."

She nodded, her expression determined. But Jake could see that she was shaking. If her jaws weren't clamped so tight he was sure her teeth would be chattering.

"Let's go," he said.

Taking her hand, he started into the swirling white void.

RASMUSSEN STOOD with his back to the brutal north wind straining to see through the whirlwind of snow. "Where the hell are they?" he said.

Derrick LeValley shook his head. "It's easy to get disoriented in this kind of weather. Let's give him a few more minutes."

"I ought to put a bullet in his brain for keeping me waiting."

"Save your bullets for the woman," LeValley said.

"My only regret is that Vanderpol won't be here to watch her die." Rasmussen checked the clip on his pistol and strode to the chopper. "You going to be able to get us out of here?"

The pilot flipped a cigarette into the snow. "It's clear just north of here. Front is blowing through, bringing some lake-effect snow. Looks worse than what it really is."

"Excellent. Be prepared for takeoff."

"Mr. Rasmussen!"

He looked at LeValley, who was pointing at two figures in the distance. "There they are."

Rasmussen narrowed his eyes. Sure enough his longtime employee and Kelsey were a hundred yards away and walking toward them. Jealousy and bitterness seared him as he watched them approach. Kelsey was the only woman he'd ever loved. But she'd betrayed him, and now he had no choice but to kill her. His only regret was Vanderpol. But if Vanderpol was under her spell, he knew the other man would suffer when he learned of her death. And in a few months, once Rasmussen was settled in a new country, he could always send someone back to finish the agent....

Withdrawing the pistol from his coat pocket, he pulled back the slide and dropped a bullet into the chamber.

"Get the chain," he told LeValley and started toward the two figures. "Let's get this nasty business over with."

JAKE COULD FEEL Leigh trembling violently as they approached Rasmussen. He could feel his own nerves crawling when he saw the pistol in the other man's hand.

"What the hell took you so long?" Rasmussen demanded.

"Lost my way in the snow," Jake said in a low voice.

Rasmussen looked at Leigh. "It looks like loverboy isn't going to save you this time."

LeValley approached them with the heavy length of chain. "We don't have much time, Mr. Rasmussen."

For a full minute Rasmussen didn't take his eyes from Leigh. With a grimace, he took her arm. "Come with me," he said.

Letting her go was the hardest thing Jake had ever done in his life. But he needed a better feel for the situation before he made his move. He needed to know how many men there were. How well they were armed. He needed to know where the chopper pilot was.

He gritted his teeth in fury when Rasmussen shoved Leigh. It took every bit of self-discipline he possessed not to go to the other man and take him apart with his bare hands. But he held his temper, if only by a thread. He needed to concentrate, get a handle on the situation and what they were up against.

At best it was three against two. Jake might be a highly trained agent, but Leigh wasn't. He could tell by the way Rasmussen was looking at her that he was near the snapping point. Jake figured he had two or three minutes before all hell broke loose.

The chopper was fifty yards away. The engine was running, the blades whipping through heavy snowfall. The pilot was already inside. Behind him, Rasmussen and the man Jake recognized as renegade U.S. marshal Derrick LeValley were taking Leigh to the hole in the ice.

Knowing he only had seconds to act, Jake went to the chopper and opened the hatch. He caught a glimpse of the pilot's face. A pistol lay on the jump seat behind him.

"You got a smoke?" Jake asked, stepping onto the foothold.

The man reached into his pocket. Jake delivered a bone crunching punch to his forehead. Then a quick upper cut to his chin. The pilot's hands flew up to protect his face. Jake finished him off with a brutal jab to the solar plexus. The pilot slumped against the seat.

Jake climbed into the chopper. Finding a bungee cord tie-down used for stowing and securing items in the fuselage, he tied the pilot's hands behind his back and heaved him into the rear.

"Sweet dreams," Jake said, and slipped out the hatch.

Chapter Twenty

Dread and horror creeping over her, Leigh stood a few feet from the opening in the ice. Even knowing one of the cuffs wasn't secure was not enough to keep the terror at bay. There were simply too many things that could go wrong.

She stood quietly while Rasmussen draped the heavy chain over her shoulders. It was incredibly heavy—at least forty or fifty pounds. If he shoved her through the hole in the ice and into the water, she wouldn't stand a chance….

Her entire body vibrated with terror. She'd lost sight of Jake in the heavily falling slow and could only assume he'd gone to the chopper. She wondered when he was going to make his move.

"I'm sorry it has come to this, my darling."

If she hadn't been so terrified, Leigh would have laughed because she knew he was just twisted enough to mean it. "Please don't do this," she choked.

"You betrayed me. Humiliated me."

"I was afraid," she said, trying to buy time.

"I lost six years of my life because of you. Six years of being treated like an animal. If I don't do this, I'll lose face." He shrugged. "You've left me no choice."

Leigh's heart pounded like a jackhammer.

"I loved you," he said.

She couldn't speak. Her breaths tore from her mouth in ragged gasps. She imagined the shock of the icy water. The black abyss closing over her.

"One last kiss goodbye, and I have to go." Never taking his eyes from hers, he leaned close.

Leigh steeled herself against the revolting press of his mouth against hers. She couldn't stop thinking of that hole in the ice just a few feet away. Of how easily he could shove her into it.

Jake, where are you?

She closed her eyes as Rasmussen made a mockery of kissing her, but she endured the intimate contact.

"Hold it right there."

Looking shocked, Rasmussen moved away. "Shoot him!" he shouted to LeValley.

Leigh looked up to see Jake standing a few yards away. He held the shotgun on Le-Valley. The pistol in his hand was directed at Rasmussen. "Move and I'll put a bullet between your eyes." He looked at Leigh. "Are you all right?"

"I'm okay," she said.

He looked at the two men. "Toss those guns now," he said menacingly.

"I hope you said your prayers last night, Vanderpol, because you're not going to live through this," Rasmussen spat.

"I'll take my chances." Jake pumped the shotgun and leveled it on the other man's chest. "Put your hands up now or I'm going to put a hole in you."

Rasmussen's and LeValley's hands went up simultaneously.

Jake's gaze flicked to Leigh. "Drop the cuffs. Get the pistol. If LeValley so much as moves I want you to put a bullet in his chest."

She didn't need to be told twice. She broke open the cuffs. Relief made her legs go weak as she began loosening the chain from around her shoulders.

The chain slipped from her left shoulder, but caught on her hips. Using both hands she tried to tug it down. A terrible guttural cry sounded. She looked up to see Rasmussen charge her, his face contorted in rage.

"You slut!" he yelled. "How dare you betray me again!"

He moved so fast Leigh didn't have time to brace. One second she was struggling to free herself from the chain. The next his hands slammed into her and she was reeling backward. She twisted in midair in an effort to avoid the hole in the ice, but the chain slipped into the water, tugging her off balance.

"Jake!" she shouted as she plunged into the water, the weight of the chain was dragging her down.

HORROR ENVELOPED JAKE as he watched Leigh go into the icy water. She was still entangled in the chain. An EMT, he knew hypothermia could render a person unconscious in a matter of minutes. The urge to go to her was powerful. But he knew if he did, the other two men would shoot them down like dogs.

Out of the corner of his eye Jake saw LeValley go for the gun he'd tossed into the snow. Jake brought up the pistol and fired twice in quick succession. LeValley clutched his stomach and hit the ice. Jake spun to see Rasmussen level the pistol at him. A gunshot exploded. Hot pain tore through his right shoulder. Jake saw blood on his coat. Blood in the snow. His right arm hung uselessly at his side.

"She's mine, Vanderpol! She was mine before she was yours."

Dizzy with pain, Jake watched Rasmussen back toward the chopper. He couldn't feel his right arm, saw blood dripping onto the snow from his fingertips. *Damn,* he thought, and wondered if he could make the shot left-handed.

"Jake. *Jake!*"

Leigh's cries tortured him. Her voice was

already getting weak, the cold zapping her strength. In his peripheral vision he could see her gripping the ice. *Hang on baby,* he thought.

Wild-eyed, Rasmussen raised the shotgun and leveled it at Jake. "Now you can watch her die."

Jake snatched the gun from the ice. It felt awkward in his left hand. Rasmussen fired. Ice kicked up inches from Jake's leg. Jake returned fire. The first shot went wide. The second struck Rasmussen in the thigh. The arms dealer went to his knees. Another gunshot exploded. Jake groaned when the bullet grazed his side. He took aim and fired three times. Rasmussen fell forward onto the ice.

Jake went to his hands and knees and crawled to the hole in the ice. "Hang on, baby. I'm here."

"J-Jake. Y-you're b-bleeding."

Her face was deathly pale, her lips tinged blue from the cold. Her gloved hands clung to the ice. He was in bad shape, but if it was the last thing he did he was going to get her out of that water.

Grinding his teeth in pain, he took her hand. "I want you to lift your foot and put it on the edge of the ice so I can pull you up."

He could tell by the way she moved that hypothermia was already setting in. As if in slow motion, she leaned back. Her face contorted with effort, but her foot never broke the surface of the water.

"Come on, honey. Work with me. Get your foot on the ice so I can pull you out of there." He could feel the warmth of blood oozing down his abdomen and prayed he stayed conscious long enough to get her out.

"Ch-chain," she whispered.

Jake didn't hesitate and plunged his left hand into the water. The chain was still entwined around her, weighing her down. Gripping it, he tugged hard, desperately trying to dislodge it from her body.

"C-can't hold on," she said.

Dizziness descended, and for a terrifying instant Jake thought he was going to pass out. "Damn it, Leigh, losing you is not an option."

"Just…hold on to me."

Her voice was so weak he could barely

make out the words. He was lying on his stomach with both arms around her. He couldn't believe after everything they'd gone through, it was going to end like this. That she was going to die in his arms because he was too damn weak to pull her out of the water. Talk about irony. They'd been so damn close....

A buzzing sounded in his ears. Jake shook his head, certain that unconsciousness was about to descend. At least they would die together....

He set his mouth close to her ear. "I love you," he whispered, pressing his mouth to her neck. "I've always loved you."

"Vanderpol! Holy frickin' cow!"

The sound of Rick Monteith's voice jerked him from semiconsciousness. Footsteps pounded on the ice behind him. He raised his head and looked around in time to see Rick charging toward him.

"About damn time," Jake ground out.

"You can sue me later."

Strong arms gripped his shoulders and dragged him back. "Can't...leave her."

But Rick was already pulling Leigh from

the hole in the ice. Even as he laid her on the snow covered ground, he was working off his coat to cover her.

"I've got you," he said. "You're going to be all right." He looked at Jake. "For God's sake, Jake, you're bleeding all over the place."

"It's not like I have a choice."

Rick rose. "Stay with her. Chopper's on the way. I've got chemical warmers in the snowmobile."

Jake had already crawled over to where Leigh lay motionless in the snow. Her face was colorless. Her lips were the deep blue of a bruise.

"Leigh," he said. "Come on, honey, wake up. Talk to me."

Her eyes fluttered open. "You saved…my life."

"Yeah, well, I had a little help."

A smile whispered across her mouth. "Did I dream that you told me you love me?"

"You didn't dream it."

"I guess this would be a good time to confess that I love you, too."

Her eyes tried to roll back, but he shook

her. "Leigh, damn it, hang on. Please, honey. I need you. There's a chopper on the way."

"…always…loved you," she whispered.

Rick returned and knelt beside Leigh. "You're going to have to let go of her, partner. Let me get these warmers against her abdomen and then I'll assess those bullet wounds."

Too weak to argue, Jake rolled onto his back and looked up at the sky. Snow swirled crazily all around. He felt Leigh's hand, cold and lifeless within his. *Please don't let her die,* he thought.

Drowsiness tugged at him, dragging him to a place that was dark and warm and safe. He thought he saw a chopper hovering overhead, but he couldn't hear the rotors and figured he must be hallucinating.

Then the darkness engulfed him. Warmth infused his body. He gripped Leigh's hand tighter. *I love you,* he thought.

But it wasn't enough to keep the darkness at bay.

Chapter Twenty-One

Jake opened one eye and for a moment wondered what he'd done to deserve ending up in heaven. He was surrounded by warmth and white and a pleasant lavender haze. A few feet away, Leigh smiled down at him, and he was suddenly very glad for all the Sundays he'd spent in church.

"C'mere." He reached for her only to be halted by the dull throb in his shoulder. The pain was the first inkling that he hadn't actually made it into heaven.

"How are you feeling?" she asked.

"Hurts," he croaked.

"The doctor said if you need something for the pain all you have to do is ask."

As far as Jake was concerned his head was fuzzy enough. "Where am I?"

"St. Francis Hospital in Detroit."

His other eye popped open. "How long?"

"Two days." She took his hand then, and Jake almost forgot about the pain.

Her hand was warm and small and incredibly soft within his. Even drugged and hurting he was aware of the need rising inside him. He wanted to kiss her and never stop, but he didn't think he was strong enough and settled for squeezing her hand. "You're a sight for sore eyes."

Leaning close, she pressed a kiss to his forehead. "So are you."

His vision clearing, he looked around the room and spotted Rick Monteith. "What about Rasmussen?"

Monteith shook his head. Dead. Jake felt nothing but relief. He recalled the final minutes on the ice. Leigh in the water and fighting for her life. He remembered Rasmussen taking a shot at him. He thought he recalled seeing a chopper.

"What happened?" he asked.

Monteith and Leigh exchanged glances. "Rasmussen put a bullet in your shoulder," Rick said. "Dislocated it. Nicked an artery.

You lost a lot of blood. Passed out. By the time the chopper arrived, you barely had a pulse."

Leigh squeezed his hand, tears glistening in her eyes. "You never let go of me, Jake. Even when you were unconscious, you refused to let go. Rick had to pry your hand off me."

Jake wasn't sure why that embarrassed him. Maybe because Rick was standing there, and he'd never been very good at showing his emotions, particularly when it came to the woman he loved more than his own life. "Yeah, well, I didn't want Monteith stealing my woman."

"All bets are off until you get your ass out of that bed, Vanderpol." Rick moved his eyebrows like Groucho Marx.

Leigh punched Rick good-naturedly in the shoulder.

"How's Madrid?" Jake asked.

"He's in the room next door," Rick said. "Nasty bullet wound in his abdomen. Had to have surgery, and it was dicey for a while. But he's going to be okay."

Jake grimaced. "Damn armor-piercing bullets are a bitch."

"Don't feel too bad for him," Rick said. "He wants to punch your lights out for thinking he sold you out."

"Yeah, well, he's going to have to wait in line," Jake said, thinking of his surly boss. "I'm sure Cutter wants his pound of flesh."

"He's looked in on you several times in the past couple of days. No one can figure out if he wants you to wake up because he's worried or if he wants to rake you over some hot coals."

"Pretty ticked off, huh?"

"You bet."

The door opened. Jake looked past Leigh and Rick to see his superior Sean Cutter enter the room. "Who's ticked off?"

Rick muttered a curse under his breath.

Cutter's gaze went to Jake and held. "Get lost, Monteith. Vanderpol and I have some business to discuss."

Monteith nodded briskly at Cutter as the two men passed each other. Cutter strode over to the bed, barely sparing Leigh a glance.

"I should probably go," she said.

Jake didn't let go of her hand. "Anything he has to say, you can hear it."

"I don't mind dressing you down in front of a civilian," Cutter said bluntly.

"Then do it," Jake returned, but he was edgy all the same. His job with the MIDNIGHT Agency meant the world to him. He could tell by the look in Cutter's eyes that he was going to fire him. Jake had broken too many rules in the past few days to count. But holding Leigh's hand in his, he knew he'd do it all over again to save her life.

He loved her. More than his job. More than his own life. Whatever transpired in the next minutes didn't really matter in the scope of things. She was the only thing he needed in his life to be happy.

Cutter scowled at Jake. "You disobeyed a direct order."

"Several," Jake muttered and mentally braced, telling himself he could always hire on as a Rent-a-Cop until he found something he could live with.

"You just about got one of my men killed. You stole a vehicle. You used your position with my agency to further a personal agenda."

Leigh stuck out her chin. "With all due respect, that agenda just happened to be my life."

Jake squeezed her hand. "Leigh—"

She ignored him, her eyes sharp on Cutter. "This man saved me from a slow and agonizing death. He stopped a dangerous criminal, and took a renegade U.S. marshal off the street. He risked his career and his very life to do the right thing."

Cutter just stared at her. Jake shifted uncomfortably in the bed, secretly proud of her, wishing Cutter would just get this over with.

"Are you finished?" Cutter asked after a moment.

Leigh blinked as if realizing she'd overstepped. "Yes," she said.

"In that case." Cutter tugged an envelope from his jacket and passed it to Jake. "This is for you."

Jake took the envelope from him and slid out the card inside. He recognized the star on the card, but couldn't quite get his mind around its significance. "What is this?"

"I nominated you for the MIDNIGHT Star award."

Jake didn't know what to say. Didn't know what to feel. Not when he'd been expecting one thing and receiving the exact opposite. The MIDNIGHT Star Award was the highest award a MIDNIGHT agent could earn.

"The ceremony is two weeks from today," Cutter said. "The Ritz-Carlton in D.C. Don't be late."

"I'll be there," Jake heard himself say.

Cutter offered his hand. "I don't necessarily agree with your methods, but you did good work, Vanderpol."

Jake took the other man's hand and shook it. "Thank you, sir."

Nodding at Leigh, Sean Cutter turned and left the room.

"Did that really just happen?" Leigh asked.

Jake grinned at her. "Unless they're pumping hallucinogens into me, I'd venture to say Cutter just let me off the hook in a very big way."

"He knows you're a good agent."

"Smart guy."

She touched the side of his face. "You look happy."

"There's only one thing that would make me happier."

"I don't think you're in any condition to—"

He laughed. "Marry me." He hadn't meant to say it, but now that the words were out he couldn't take them back. He didn't want to.

Color bloomed in her cheeks.

"If I could get down on one knee I would," he added.

"I'm going to hold you to that." She put a trembling hand to her mouth. "Jake…"

"I love you," he said. "I want to spend the rest of my life with you. I want to wake up with you every morning and go to sleep with you every night. I want to make you happy."

Tears glittered in her eyes, and for a split second he was terrified she was going to say no. "Honey, don't cry."

"I'm not." She blinked, and they spilled over her lashes.

Jake didn't argue. "If this is happening too fast—"

"It's not. I've waited six years for this."

"I've been waiting my entire life," he whispered.

"Well then, we'd better not waste any more time," she said.

Smiling, he reached over with his good arm and pulled her close for a long kiss.

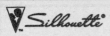

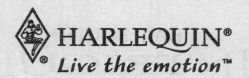
HARLEQUIN®
Live the emotion™

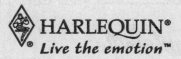